FAKING CHRISTMAS LOVE AT THE DOGGY SPA

A SWEET ROMANTIC COMEDY

FINDING LOVE AT THE DOGGY SPA

ELSIE WOODS

ISBN : 978-2-492606-09-0

Achevé d'imprimer en décembre 2021

Prix : 6€

CLAIRE

"I absolutely cannot procure candles in the shape of Santa's face that sparkle red and green!"

I shout into my Bluetooth earbud, not because I'm annoyed but because my boss is a seventy-five-year-old former rockstar who refuses to believe he has hearing loss.

"My wife tells me they are all the rage this year!"

Cornelius barks at my feet. He doesn't trust the elves who serve at Santa's workshop in the mall. I can't blame him. Santa is one thing, but a bunch of grown-ups dressed as elves? I've got my limits on this Christmas stuff.

Cornelius growls like he's a big scary beast, when he's actually a nine-pound wiener dog. Nine pounds of barky, sparky love, as I like to say.

I wait for Mr. Denudo to finish ranting about the importance of red and green sparkling candles while I battle the crowds to the sound of carols. It's five days before Christmas and three days before the Huxton Christmas Extravaganza. And that means that I'm going crazy with thousands of people to witness it up and down the corridors between shops, stands, and pop-up hot chocolate tables for charity.

"I'm telling you, sir," I shout over the carolers, "I have been up and down these shops – and by the way, do you know how hard that is five days before Christmas – and nowhere, anywhere is there…"

Wait a second. That stall across from the calendar store.

"Hang on, Mr. D."

"Claire, I am absolutely certain that red and green sparkling Santa heads are exactly what we need to ensure the Huxtons are wowed this year. I don't have to tell you how many clients will be there."

It's sitting on the table in front of me, and I can hardly believe it. I pick up the life-size Santa head molded out of wax.

Gosh darn it, Mr. D. was right.

"Sparkling Santa head candles. I'm on it, Mr. D. I'll pick up ten."

"Make it twenty!"

Twenty life-size wax Santa heads. I'm not gonna lie, it's a little creepy. But Mr. Denudo's wife was right. They are all the rage.

A teenager helping his mom run the stall pushes the cart with the boxes of candles, because Santa heads are remarkably heavy.

"Watch your step," I call back to him, nearly at my Trailblazer. The ground is slick with wet snow, the kind that doesn't stick but instead turns a parking lot into a mucky ice rink. The last thing I need is a liability suit right now.

Colorado in winter. The piles of snow are high on the sides, but thankfully the city of Hampton Falls knows how to clear the way for shoppers, skiers, and celebrities alike. I just hope there will be a dusting for Christmas Eve. I could do without all the hype of the holiday, but snow at Christmas is magic.

"What do you need so many heads for?" he asks me while

skidding carefully with the load. "Most people are happy with one."

"You haven't met my boss. Everything is all about ensuring the clients pick us for their event. And if that means twenty sparkling Santa heads, so be it."

Mr. Denudo and his events. I've got to give the guy credit. He's old school, but people trust him because of it. 'High integrity, high performance, high rock 'n roll' is the slogan of Rockin' Event Promotions. After spending twenty-five years as a rockstar heartthrob back in the day, he sure managed to find some transferable skills.

As for me, I'm still waiting for that MBA to pay itself off.

I knew it would take time, and my parents tried to talk me out of doing so many years of school, but the truth is that I loved it. I loved the studying, I loved the business, I loved finding unusual solutions to complex problems.

I just didn't think that it would involve a trunk full of sparkling Santa heads.

I slam the trunk shut and pass the kid a ten dollar bill.

"Wow! That's so generous. Come back anytime!"

"Hopefully I've got all the heads I need, but you have a merry Christmas now."

After strapping Cornelius into his car seat, we're off, slip-sliding our way through the overcrowded parking lot toward the HQ of Rockin' Event Promotions.

I hear a noise from the seat beside me. A noise that doesn't belong in a dog.

"Was that a cough?" I look at my dachshund. He looks back at me like I'm crazy so I roll on forward.

I hear the cough again.

"I heard that, Cornelius!" I pull the car over into a spot that just opened.

"I was waiting for that spot!" a woman calls from the car facing me.

"I'll just be a second, I think my dog is sick!"

"Oh no! Your dog? You take care of that, dear." She smiles at me and winds her window back up.

Thank goodness for Christmas spirit.

Cornelius is still looking at me like nothing happened. It's a showdown. I'm staring at him, he's staring at me. His mouth is tightly shut and his bulging eyes are even bulgier than usual.

I know he's trying to hold it back. His eyes are watering.

"Just let it out, little man."

He coughs.

"I knew it! That's it, we're calling Dr. Chamberlain."

Dr. Chamberlain. Only the cutest vet on this side of the Rocky Mountains with his bushy beard and rugged good looks…

Not that I noticed.

I used to take Cornelius to your regular, uninteresting, decidedly average-looking vet in town. But when my bestie Amelia got hooked up as a dog groomer at the Dog's Paw Dog Spa, I had to give them my business, right?

And I wouldn't trust my little sausage to just anyone. Did I mention that Dr. Chamberlain has a degree from Harvard?

Regardless of Dr. Chamberlain's hunky exterior, when I see him, it's all business. Especially a day like today with Mr. Denudo breathing down my neck and nearly two hundred big clients coming to the Huxton Christmas. There's a lot riding on it, including my future promotion. In theory, I don't have time for a visit to the vet.

But in reality, I'll do anything for Cornelius.

He may not look like much, being a nine-pound ankle-biter (figuratively, as he's the sweetest pup around). But he's my best friend – Amelia notwithstanding. He's there for me every morning and every night. He will protect me to the death, I have no doubt of that.

And given that trying to maintain a romantic relationship while preparing to take over the largest event management agency in this part of the country is impossible, Cornelius is all I've got.

He coughs again.

"Hang in there, little man." I dial up the Dog's Paw on Bluetooth.

"Hello and welcome to the Dog's Paw Dog Spa where it is always a waggingly wonderful day. How can I help you?"

"Rita, it's Claire."

"Claire! It's been ages. Let me get Amelia for you–"

"Actually I need an emergency appointment with Dr. Chamberlain."

"Oh no, something wrong with little Corny?"

"He's coughing!" I feel myself choke up in spite of myself.

"You just come on over. We'll fit you in between Prince Gregory and Magic."

"Thank you, Rita. Thank you." I grip the wheel tighter and blink away tears as Cornelius coughs again.

The Dog's Paw Dog Spa is only about fifteen minutes outside of town, but the moment the high rises turn to houses and houses turn to evergreens, there's something magical that happens. The hotel beside the Dog's Paw caters to the rich and famous, and it's easy to see why. Nestled in the mountains, surrounded by trees, in a stately home that rivals the White House, what celebrity wouldn't want to come here for a getaway?

Especially when they can bring their pooch along with them.

I park badly between two spots but as close to the door as possible. The entry to the Dog's Paw is all glass, and through it I can see Christmas at its finest. Garlands of evergreen branches strung with little white lights and red ribbons, a tree covered in bone-shaped ornaments in gold and red.

Music is coursing out of an invisible speaker into the parking lot, and if it weren't for Cornelius coughing, this would be the most idyllic moment of the season.

Through the window, I see Dr. Chamberlain. He smiles and waves like we're old friends. Lab coat and glasses on, he somehow radiates warmth and friendliness.

I bite my lip and smile back.

My phone rings.

Christmas for event planners is like New Year's Eve in Times Square. No time for rest.

"Sorry, Mr. D., I have to take Cornelius to the vet, I'll call you back." I wrangle Cornelius into the Dog's Paw Dog Spa, where a little pug rushes over to give Cornelius a sniff.

"It's about that illuminated backdrop for the stage…"

Amelia enters the reception area and gives a little wave. I mouth "Give me a minute" to Amelia.

"I'll call you back, sir." I hang up on Mr. D. He doesn't like when I do that, but desperate times call for desperate measures. I take in a deep breath, and so does Cornelius, except that he coughs it all back out.

"Oh no, I heard that, little guy." Amelia comes over and makes a worried face while holding Cornelius' snout in her hands. "You switched to the food I suggested, didn't you? His coat looks great." Amelia smiles at me and must see the panic in my eyes because she immediately changes tack. "Aw, hun. Are you that worried? Dr. Chamberlain will fix him up in no time."

"What if it's his heart?" I manage to choke out.

"Hey, hey."

Amelia puts her hands on my arms and already I'm feeling reassured. Amelia is going to be a vet one day if all goes to plan, and she's like the dog whisperer crossed with Mother Theresa. Given all she's gone through in her life, that's saying a lot.

"Let me get Tom for you."

"Tom?" I gawk. "I have to see Dr. Chamberlain. No one but Dr. Chamberlain!" I think I'm going to faint.

Amelia laughs. "Tom *is* Dr. Chamberlain. He has a first name, you know? And a really nice place on the edge of town… and a great sense of humor…"

There's a glint in her eye. I don't get it.

She waves her hand. "Never mind. Sometimes I forget that you're a career woman with a soft spot for wiener dogs."

"That's the pot calling the kettle black." I give her a look she knows well. Amelia and I have that in common. Determination, perseverance, success at all costs.

Except with our puppies. Dogs are always the exception.

"Sit on down. I'll check if Dr. Chamberlain is ready for you." She winks.

Why would she do that?

TOM

My phone dings with a text.

"No excuses, this year we are meeting her. You promised. Tell this mystery woman who's won your heart that she's stopping by for dinner on the 23rd. That's not even Xmas. No excuses."

My head is starting to hurt.

I had a whole year to break up with my fake girlfriend, and I didn't do it. What was I thinking?

It made sense two years ago that she didn't come to my sister's Christmas Day event. After all, we'd only just started dating. Fake dating that is. Is it fake dating if the person doesn't even exist? Or is it just a pretend girlfriend?

Last year it was because fake-pretend-girlfriend had important family stuff to do, and we'd only been together a year.

Then it was easier to keep up the charade all year, keeping my loving-but-nosy family off my back. But it's been two years now and "she" hasn't met my family yet.

Now what?

I can't dump my pretend girlfriend the week before

Christmas, that's unfeeling. My sister would never forgive me.

"She" could dump me… I'd have to show some emotion about it after the way I've talked her up, and I've never been good at feelings-on-command.

Fortunately, I don't have much time to think about it, as an English bulldog with an evil looking grimace comes waddling into my examination room.

"I'm telling you, Dr. Chamberlain," his human begins, "it came out of nowhere. Russel is the sweetest animal on the planet and now he's in a perpetual snarl at me. It's like the devil's got hold of him!"

Actresses. Hermione Aiden is one of the Chateau Rose Hotel's most distinguished guests, so I can't shrug her off. Still, she inevitably finds something wrong with her slobbery, overweight English Bulldog during each stay at the hotel.

Russel a fine specimen of the breed, white and brown, with a face that says, "Don't mess with me."

Though I think even he is getting a touch fed up by his master's coddling.

That being said, he does have an awkward snarl. That's not the Russel I know. The Russel I know goes with the punches, waddles his way through life, doing as he pleases.

Russel is not a snarler.

"Let me check his glands." I snap on a pair of gloves. "Blocked glands just might be enough to make ol' Russ here uncomfortable."

"Glands? Like in his throat?"

"No." I reach in where I have to in order to check.

"Russ has glands *there*?"

"All dogs do, ma'am."

"Goodness, call me Hermione already. Given your –" she whirls her hand in the air over the dog's backside "–close relationship with Russel, I think we can be on a first name basis."

"His glands are fine, which is good news. He's still too young for that kind of trouble."

I step back and look the dog in the eye. If I didn't know better, I'd say he was rebuking me for not finding the source of his trouble. His lip trembles, curls up. Highly unnatural.

Hermione holds her head in her hands. "Ever since I told him off for marching through the hotel's rose bushes, he hasn't been the same."

"Rose bushes, huh?"

I have an idea.

"Gorgeous Christmas roses that are coming up in the beds in the back garden. I was so ashamed! But if I'd known, I wouldn't have shouted so loudly at him. He hates shouting!"

Do I tell her she's shouting now? In any case, I believe I'm about to solve the mystery of the snarling bulldog. "Rose bushes. Big slobbery dog in rose bushes…"

"Who are you calling slobbery?"

I reach into his mouth, confident now that the snarl is not any kind of aggression, but rather an attempt to save himself from discomfort.

"Ta-da! This is the villain!" I hold out my hand, now well covered in slippery saliva, and show the inch-long rose thorn that had been lodged between Russel's teeth.

"Russel! Oh, my baby!" She takes him in her arms. "Thank goodness you're okay. That was a close one, a real close one. Imagine if you really had been transformed into a mean doggie?"

There was nothing close about it. He had something lodged between his teeth. But I don't feel like making a deal out of it. I have another patient waiting for me.

And that's the patient I want to see.

What am I saying? Claire Ingram is just a client, the owner of a cheeky dachshund, nothing more than that.

Amelia pops her head in. "Your favorite client is here."

I look at her over the rim of my glasses. "I assume you mean Cornelius."

"Whatever…"

"You just 'whatever' your way back to the waiting room and send them in."

She gives me a sly smile, though she knows I am an utmost professional. Always have been. That's what set me apart at grad school. The others could be off partying, I saved it for summer holidays. When the weather turned cooler, that was work time.

"Dr. Chamberlain." Claire rushes in with the dog in her arms and her normally very tidy hair now in a bun that's gone askew. A few strands fall across her face. She brushes them aside. "It just started today. I hope I've come soon enough. I can't bear to imagine it's something serious. But the cough–"

As if on cue, the dog coughs.

"You see what I mean?" Her brown eyes are wide in distress. I don't think I've ever wanted so badly to comfort a client. She's on the verge of tears.

"You did the right thing. We're going to get Cornelius all sorted out." I turn to the wee canine. I don't normally find sausage dogs special, but this little guy is different. I'm used to seeing benevolence in Labradors, some shepherds, and the occasional boxer. But in a Dachshund, it's pretty rare.

I do the classic examination, a little massage of the trachea. That alone sets Cornelius off on another chain of hacking cough.

"Oh, Corny!" Claire cries.

"That's good news." I love being able to be the bearer of good news. Especially to such sad brown eyes - and I don't mean Corny's. "If it only started today, and considering that he responded to my touch, we can be pretty confident it's tracheobronchitis and nothing more serious than that."

She looks doubtful. "Tracheobronchitis sounds serious."

"It's kennel cough."

"Oh." She stands up straighter and lets out a big sigh. "Kennel cough. Thank goodness."

I pat the little guy on the head. "We'll do a blood test to cover all the bases. I'll get Rita at reception to sort out the antibiotics and we'll do a follow up in a couple of days to be sure." I awkwardly tap the script into my tablet. I've never been great at this tech stuff.

Her shoulders relax and her eyes flutter closed. "You don't know how much this means to me."

Without thinking, I reach out I touch her shoulder. "I do know. They are family."

She opens her eyes and smiles at me. "Yes. Family."

In that moment we both realize that my hand is still on her shoulder and now it's reached the point where it's awkward if I leave it and awkward if I remove it. What do I?

She's the one who decides.

She stands up, clears her throat and extends her hand.

"Thank you, doctor. A most helpful and reassuring visit."

I shake her hand. It feels weird, a moment ago we were so much closer.

"My pleasure." At least I found normal-person words to say. I was beginning to worry there. "Rita will sort out Cornelius' medication and payment. For the appointment. The appointment today."

That was less normal. Get it together, Tom.

But tripping over my words makes her smile.

Her phone rings. She answers it on the little Bluetooth earphone that I hadn't seen tucked behind her copper-colored hair.

"Yes, Mr. D." Her voice is completely changed, no more the worried dog mama, now she's all business. "I can prepare those invoices before the Huxton event. Shall we include the French dancers to go with the Provençal cuisine? – Yes, certainly, it would be most appropriate for the Huxton event, they do like things to be inclusive. My plus one? Of course – No, I won't bring him again, don't worry. I had no idea he had such a sugar addiction. – I'll let you know as soon as I – Yes, sir – Yes, sir."

She ends the call with a dramatic tap on the screen.

"Sorry, I'll get out of here. I'm sure you have other patients waiting."

"Sounds like you've got quite a season ahead of you."

"Tis the season, especially for event planners."

"And you need a plus–" I stop myself. What am I saying? Why am I getting in the middle of her business?

"Have a great day, Dr. Chamberlain."

And just like that, she's gone.

I peek out the door just in time to catch a glimpse of her chatting with Amelia. Her back is to me, but Amelia catches me watching. She raises an eyebrow.

I have to tell Amelia that this is all innocent. Claire – I mean, Ms. Ingram – is just a client. A friendly, interesting, smart, beautiful client. That's all.

Claire heads to the reception desk with Cornelius trotting behind, and Amelia walks my way.

"I don't want to hear it," is all I say.

She lifts her hands as if to show she's weaponless. "I wasn't going to say anything, doctor."

"Good." I cross my arms and catch Claire smiling at Rita as she swivels to leave. She and I briefly make eye contact and I muster a shy grin.

Amelia is still standing in front of me, head cocked to the

side. I take in a deep breath and address her. "Don't you have a client yourself?"

"I have a break before Mitzi. And it's just as well, I'm looking at vet school applications."

"Yes! Good on you, Amelia. You'll have to tell me which ones you're looking at. But later. I believe I have another patient." I scroll through the tablet but still cannot figure out how to see which patient is next.

"Yes," Amelia laughs, "you certainly do."

I don't know what's so funny about that until I hear a voice down the corridor.

"DOCTOR CHAMBERLAAAAIIIIIINNNNN!"

"It's Mrs. Banks?" I whisper at Amelia, "Why didn't you warn me?"

"I tried." She shrugs and walks in the other direction. "You were distracted."

"DOCTOOOOOOOOR!"

Mrs. Banks and her Great Dane, Werbel, canter down the hall in my direction. Like owner like dog, they take up all the space, bounding as though their lives depended on it. When I first met them, I was intimidated by the sight. A Great Dane is a big dog, but beside Mrs. Banks, Werbel looks like an overgrown chihuahua.

"Hello, Werbel. And hello, Mrs. Banks. Lovely to see you, as always. Did Werbel eat a spatula again?"

"The oven mitt!"

CLAIRE

"I'm serious, Amelia. These are events where the plus one is a sign of status. If I go on my own, then I look like hired help."

I can practically hear Amelia rolling her eyes over the speakerphone. "This is why I stick to animals."

I'm pasting silver strands of sequins along a sign that says "Huxton Christmas" which will be the backdrop on stage for the event. I'm hoping it'll be far enough that no one will be able to see my lack of glue gun skills. I had to clear the entire kitchen floor to lay out this larger-than-life sign.

"So give me the dirt, who are the eligible bachelors?" I readjust the sequin strand that risks spelling 'Hoxton' if I'm not careful.

"I'm not doing this, Claire."

"What do you mean, you're not doing this?"

"You chew men up."

I drop the glue gun.

"I do what? Ouch!" Hot glue, on my middle finger. I run to the sink but bring the phone with me.

"You chew them up. Remember Marvin last year?"

"That was not my fault. You never told me he had a dessert problem."

"You made him so nervous!"

"It was an important event! All I said was, 'Be normal. Don't act weird. People are judging you.' He nodded like he was totally fine with that before going to town on the tiramisu cups."

Amelia sighs.

I retake my seat on the floor. "Why the sigh? It's just a fact."

She continues. "And what about Brad?"

"Brad, the sniffer? What's he got, a permanent case of allergies? He couldn't finish a sentence without making this massive suction noise between his nostrils. All I said to him was–"

"Are you not seeing the pattern?"

"Of you sending me dud guys for my classy work events? Cornelius! Cornelius! Oh no."

He's trudged along the top of the sign where the glue wasn't quite dry and the line of sequins is now following him out of the kitchen. He flees when yelled at, but I can't let him ruin the whole sign!

"Stop right there." I pick him up and unstick the strand from his little paw pad. "Now go play with your squirrel, the one you already pulled the stuffing from. Go on then."

I trudge back to the kitchen.

"You still there? Amelia?"

"I'm here."

"Minor sequin crisis. Now, where were we?"

"Find your own plus one!"

"You can't leave me like this, Amelia!" I cry into the phone's speaker. She has to know how much this matters to me, for my career. "You know I have no time to meet men in this job, and I'm so close to promotion, so close!"

"You'll figure it out, Clairibell. You have an MBA after all. Gotta go, Max rolled in chewing gum. Again."

Max, her pug puppy. He's adorable but loves rolling in anything sticky or stinky. I lucked out with Cornelius on that front. He's too snobby to roll in gunk.

But I did *not* luck out on a date for the Huxton event.

I hear the trotting of little nails on the tile.

"Say, Cornelius, I don't suppose you could shapeshift and be my date this Christmas season?"

He cocks his head.

"I promise there'd be plenty to eat…"

That makes him wag his tail, but alas, he remains – as ever – a sausage dog.

"Alright, I'll get you a treat."

PULLING INTO THE DRIVEWAY AT THE DOG'S PAW DOG SPA lightens the load. It's easy to forget the bustling city when out here. Amelia lives with her aunt in the adjacent town of Angelville, but that's way too quiet for my speed. I need the activity of a medium-sized city like Hampton Falls.

Still, breathing that fresh air and seeing the classy Christmas decorations all over the Chateau Rose hotel and the Dog's Paw beside it fills me with something different from the everyday.

Maybe it's peacefulness. Yes, the air definitely smells like peacefulness.

The waiting room is bustling today. Poor Rita has two phones going and there's at least six animals of various varieties in the room. Dogs, cats, a rabbit, a rat. Cornelius growls at the rat. You can take the dog out of the rat-hunt, but you can't take the rat-hunter out of the dog. That's what I always say. He killed one once and left it in the middle of the living room, pride painted across his little face. Yuck.

"Hi, Rita."

"Hi," she whispers with her hand across the phone receiver. "Crazy client, hang on." She clears her throat. "Yes, Mrs. Banks. Dr. Chamberlain assured me that every trace of the oven mitt was removed and that Werbel should have no trouble doing his business anymore."

"Good afternoon, lovelies!" a man calls while strutting into the waiting room. "Where's Montley? I have him scheduled for a private training session."

"Here! We're here." An older lady with a droopy-faced bloodhound stands up. "Come on, Montley." The dog looks very comfortable, imitating a rug in the middle of the waiting room floor. "It's time."

Montley doesn't budge.

The trainer stands with his hands on his hips, a short and dainty man dressed to the nines, as if he were going to a fashion show and not the arena out back for training. The only dead giveaway are his knee-high boots covered in mud.

"Julio," Rita gives his a scathing look, "you're dropping caked mud on my floor."

"Alright, alright." Julio raises his hands. "I know how to deal with this situation." He makes a grand gesture of reaching into his hip pack and opening a little baggy.

Whatever is in that baggy gets Montley up off the floor and sitting in front of Julio in half a second.

"I thought so. Reward-based training for you!"

"Miss Ingram?"

I whip my head around so fast that I see stars. Through the stars is Dr. Chamberlain's smiling face.

"You and Cornelius can come in now."

I'm two steps down the hallway when my phone rings. I

answer on speakerphone as my hands are full with Cornelius who is wriggling to watch a toy poodle strutting by.

"Guest list, Claire," Mr. Denudo warns, "I need it tomorrow morning."

"It's all set, sir. Just waiting on one confirmation."

"I don't suppose that would be your date."

"Gotta go, sir. I promise to have it with you in the morning."

I set Cornelius down on the metal table, which he hates, and hang up the phone. "Sorry about that. Work complications."

"A date to a Christmas event is a work complication? That's a first."

"You have no idea."

If only I could find someone like Dr. Chamberlain. Friendly, intelligent, good personal hygiene…

A knock on the door and it opens, Amelia's face peeking in. Cornelius' tail wags like crazy at the sight of her.

"Hey, little guy." She scratches the place under his chin that he loves. "My next client is waiting for me, so I'll be brief." She looks at Dr. Chamberlain. "You've got a sister to placate." She looks at me. "You need a plus one." She closes the door saying, "I'll let that sit with you both."

I measure up this veterinary specimen before me. Was Amelia suggesting what I think she was suggesting?

We both talk at the same time.

"I have this work thing–"

"I've got this problem–"

"You first." I set Cornelius on the floor before he jumps with reckless disdain off the table.

Dr. Chamberlain takes a deep breath and scratches the back of his head.

"I've gotten myself into a conundrum."

"Conundrum, huh? Is it that you're stuck in the Victorian England? I didn't know people still said conundrum."

He blinks. Oh crap. Is this what Amelia meant about chewing men up?

"I'm sorry." I think I might be blushing. "I cut you off. Trying to lighten the mood with a joke. You were saying?"

"Right." He sits on the edge of his desk. "I've got a problem. My sister wants – no, *demands* – that I bring my girlfriend to meet everyone on Christmas Day."

I'm failing to see why Amelia thought Dr. Chamberlain could help me with my problem if he's got a girlfriend. Maybe he can introduce me to someone?

"I see. And I'm guessing your family is quite… um…"

"Overzealous."

"I get you. That can be hard to manage. But fortunately, part of my MBA was on relationship negotiation. Normally it's the business relationship side of things, but there is a lot of cross-over to real life. I can help you."

He scratches his head again. "I'm not sure you've understood…"

"Overzealous, imposing, perhaps even meddling family. I get it. I can help you both to navigate it. Now, do you know somebody – somebody *normal* – who can be my plus one to a series of events coming up? He'll have to be ready to really act like my date. That's gone wrong in the past and I have some of my own relationship – business relationship – repairs to do because of it. But the events are fun, free food – if he goes light on the dessert – and I promise to make great company. If it's someone who wants to rub shoulders with Hampton Falls' up and coming and rich and famous and both well-liked and well-hated, then this is the gig for him."

I let out my breath. That was quite a sell. But considering that a part of me is horrified to be asking my dog's vet to hook me up with one of his buddies, it's the best I could do.

"Well," he nods his head, thinking. "I don't know about that last part, but I do have someone who is as normal as one could expect in the circumstances."

"Perfect!" I can practically see all my troubles are floating away. "Who is it?"

"Me." He smiles and opens his arms like it's obvious.

That was not what I was expecting. "You? But your girlfriend."

"There is no real girlfriend."

Oh. Now I get it.

This changes things.

TOM

Her right eyebrow raised and her lips parted a little, I wonder how far down in her esteem I've just dropped.

"So…" she begins, squinting off into the distance like she's putting the pieces together. My heart thumps between my ears. "You invented a girlfriend to get your family off your back."

"That's right."

"No real girlfriend then?"

"No real girlfriend."

She tips her head left and right as though weighing the options. "Well, at least that would mean it's less likely she would make a scene at one of my events for taking you as my plus one."

It hadn't occurred to me that my pretend girlfriend could pose a threat. "You're safe."

"Thank heavens. Because I really need less drama at these events, not more." She leans against the examination table, but before I can warn her it has wheels, she's sprawled out on the floor and Cornelius is barking up a storm.

"Whoa! Careful now." I lift her up.

"Thank you, doctor."

The way she says 'doctor' sends a shiver down my spine.

…And now we're at that awkward place again where I'm still holding her even though she's upright and if I let go, it's weird, but I certainly can't keep holding her. Not with my pretend girlfriend still to discuss.

I let her go.

Rita opens the door. "Everything okay in here? I heard a loud crash."

"Oh," Claire waves it off. "That was just my dignity tumbling to the ground. Nothing to see here."

"Ah, all good then." She smiles and leaves us back in the same awkward place we were a moment earlier.

"Calm, Cornelius. I'm fine, see?" She picks him up and snuggles her face into him.

"Look," I muster with as much courage as I can, "how about we talk this through over coffee. Purely business discussion, that is."

"Great idea." She checks her phone. "I'm free at four-fifteen for thirty minutes or six o'clock to six forty."

"That's highly specific."

"Tis the season. Meet me at Café Java?"

"Perfect."

THESE PAST THREE HOURS HAVE BEEN THE SLOWEST IN THE history of time.

I am a grown man. I have done many years of higher education. Why does coffee to talk about my fake love life freak me out so much, then?

In any case, this is what I'm doing. I am going to convince this girl – I mean, woman, it's probably condescending to call a woman with an MBA a 'girl', but she's cute as an eight-week-old labrador - I'm going to convince her to pretend to be my girlfriend with my nosy, enthusiastic family.

And in return, I'm going to be her normal plus one.

Then we can break up before New Year's and call it square. It all seems very reasonable until I'm ordering my cappuccino and see her walk through the door with the sausage dog in tow..

Now I feel like a total dweeb. Do people still say 'dweeb'? Where did I learn my slang from anyway, reruns of I Love Lucy?

I probably shouldn't tell her about my secret obsession with I Love Lucy. That might kick me squarely out of the 'normal' category.

"Hey," she says, taking off her coat. There's a big bruise forming on her arm. She catches me looking. "Yeah. Go figure that the examination table was on rollers. Fortunately, my holiday dresses are mostly long sleeved."

"Sorry about that."

"Not your fault. So… I'm gonna grab myself a coffee – seeing as you've already bought one for yourself – and I'll be right back." She hands me Cornelius' leash.

"Hiya, little man. Glad to see you're on the mend."

He wags in reply.

I should have waited and bought her coffee. D'oh. That would have been the polite thing to do when on a non-date with a potential fake girlfriend. Have I been out of the game that long? There was that girl two years ago, though she took off pretty quick for New York when she landed the role on Broadway. I really thought there was potential there, lots of little dogs in NYC, but once she said goodbye, that really had been it.

It sure has been a while. I'm guessing things have changed.

But buying the girl a coffee? That hasn't changed. I'm a dufus. Dufus… is that another one of those outdated terms?

"There we go. I just love how Kari makes a cappuccino, don't you?" She blows on the hot coffee, swirling the four-leaf clover of foam into a two-leaf clover.

"Kari, the blonde one?"

"She's the best. And did you know that Rita has been inventing new cakes for the café?"

"I did not."

"They are delish, you have to try one sometime." Her smile is glowing.

It really wouldn't be hard to pretend to like this girl. I mean, woman.

She takes a loud sip and sets the coffee down. "Here's the deal."

She just turned businesswoman. It happened before my eyes. Her spine straightened and the sparkle in her eye turned into a flame. I could get burned by a woman with such an intense gaze.

My palms are sweating.

"I have plans, big plans, for taking over Rockin' Event Promotions. This is my chance to make good on this MBA, which you can imagine did not come cheap, nor easy."

I point my thumbs at myself. "Med school. I get it." I look at my thumbs. I look like a dork.

"Yes," she continues as if I hadn't spoken, "I'll need you to both look and act the part. These are high society events, and the point is not that I'm one of them – because I'm not – but I have to show that I can create an environment that will suit their social *milieu*. Do you see what I mean?"

"I believe I do."

She twists the cup on the table, relieving me for a minute from that gaze. I realize now what it is that makes me so nervous under her watchful eye.

She's judging me.

She looks up, and that confirms it. Her eyes narrow like I'm a racehorse and she's considering putting all her money on me. "I don't want to expect any more from you than you are capable of producing, but I assure you that I am ready to do whatever it is that needs to be done with your sister and 'overzealous' family if you can help me look good in front of these clients and my boss."

"Sounds very reasonable."

She sighs. "These people are not very reasonable. And I have a track record working against me. This is where you really come in."

Sweaty palms, sweaty palms. "Okay…"

She tilts her head and her eyes relax, as if she's remembering. "Mr. Denudo gave me this job before I finished school. He took a chance on me then, but I've proven myself every step of the way. Now the problem is that he won't take me seriously. To him, I'm still the young girl getting through college." She looks me straight in the eye. "I'm not that girl anymore. I am the woman with a career in front of her that's waiting to begin and can't because I'm viewed as the person I was five years ago. That's where you can help."

"I can?"

I try to swallow a sip of cappuccino but it's nearly cold now.

"The Huxton event is our biggest one of the season. December twenty-second. Anyone who's anyone in the region will be coming, including many of the big names staying at the Chateau Rose. I'd bet you know some of their dogs. If I can pull this off, if I can make it the greatest Christmas event they've ever had, I'm sure the Huxtons will put in a strong word for my promotion to General Manager."

"Sounds easy."

"You don't know this clientele." She rubs her forehead.

"There will be a thousand things that will go wrong from Moët being served instead of Veuve Clicquot, and don't get me started on the controversy created by last year's foie gras. You will have to be the pillar helping me navigate all of that, keeping your cool and helping me keep mine, all the while not pigging out on tiramisu."

"I'm not a fan of whipped cream."

She sits back in her chair, giving me that eye again like I might not be up to this challenge.

"Not a fan of whipped cream. Do you have anything else to say for yourself?"

I have to rise to her level. This is not a simple arrangement of 'come hang with me and I'll hang with you'. It's just as well, because my sister will give her a run for her money, and I'll need her to be onside each step of the way.

Something to say for myself.

"Yes, as a matter of fact, I do."

She smiles slyly. "I'm all ears, doctor."

Doctor.

My stomach does that funny thing again.

CLAIRE

So far so good. He hasn't gone running for the hills and he hasn't accused me of being neurotic. Not yet, anyway.

In fact, he's the picture of calm, cool, and collected. Though he does seem to be holding his coffee cup too tight.

Something to say for yourself. That was probably a bit much. Makes me think that maybe Amelia wasn't totally off base with her claims of my man-chewing. I'll have to watch out. This isn't the event planning world, he's just a guy.

Actually, he's not *just a guy*. He's a nice guy. And a vet. A guy who loves dogs. That's a good place to start.

He takes a deep breath. I'm about to discover what it is he has 'to say for himself'.

"Let me lay out for you what I need from this – um – arrangement."

There's a touch of assertion in his voice now. I sit against the back of my chair with cappuccino in hand. "Please," I invite, "my curiosity is killing me. Just how *does* a handsome vet wind up creating an imaginary girlfriend to satisfy his family's meddling?"

His eyebrows flick upwards and I can tell that I've destabilized him. I was trying to be funny, but I don't think it worked. I lean forward on the table.

"What I mean is, take it away. I'm listening."

His shoulders relax.

Wow, this is a lot more effort than I thought. Who knew I could be so insensitive? I guess that's what happens when the only warm body I cuddle at night is Cornelius.

"It all began a couple of years ago. My sister was having her second kid. My older sister. I've always been happy for her, finding the man and the life she always wanted." He looks over my head. "But then the conversation became all about me. Finding me a wife. Setting me up for good. Settling me down. Next thing I knew, my sister, my cousins, even my neighbor – they were setting me up on blind dates."

"That's thoughtful."

"It was awful!" He throws his head back and I can perfectly see the boy he once was. He might be a fully grown man now, but the twinkle of rebellion in his eye is not so well masked. "I had to find a way to get them to stop. The women they were introducing me to… we had nothing in common. They were nice enough – mostly – but do you have any idea how hard it is to turn nice women down on a weekly basis?"

"It must have been *so hard* for you." Hmm, that was a tinge of sarcasm in my voice. At least it doesn't seem like he noticed.

He pauses a long moment, sips his coffee, and then looks me straight in the eye.

"I don't want to date just any girl. I want *the* girl."

Why did my heart just stop for a second?

I didn't know they made guys like this anymore. I guess he comes from a different age. It goes with his vocabulary. *Conundrum.*

I swallow hard. "That all sounds reasonable enough. How did you end up in this position then?"

He musses his dark brown hair. "Because while I know what I want, I'm not great at saying it. They were coming from a good place. They wanted the best for me. And it made them *so happy* when I told them I met someone."

"Except…"

"Except she wasn't real."

"Ah yes. Now we come to the heart of it."

He visibly grows sheepish. Who knew a six-foot tall dude who finished med school could get so embarrassed?

"I had plans to end things with her – the imaginary girl, that is – but it was easier to let it slide by. My family knows I keep this sort of thing private. So I just reassured them that all was going well but that I wasn't ready to commit to anything more serious yet. It's such an age-old line that men use, it was easy for them to buy it."

He takes another long sip and makes a face.

"It's cold. You want another?"

He strides over to the counter, which gives me time to measure him up. He's a ball of contradictions. Self-assured and self-conscious. Wise and impulsive. Handsome and… well, just handsome. I can't even bring myself to use the word hot, because there is something refined about him. He's handsome, in the old-fashioned sense of the word. Hand-some, smart, classy.

He walks back to the table with two steaming cups in hand. "There you go. And a little treat for Cornelius."

"Kari always was partial to him."

I look down at my coffee to find a heart drawn in the foam. I look over to Kari who winks. I give her a look that I hope tells her she's got it all wrong.

"You were saying?" I slurp the heart away.

"I was saying that while you have certain needs and

expectations from me, I've got the same from you – though different."

I set my coffee cup with a clink on the table.

Now we're getting down to business.

"Tell me."

He goes through a laundry list of family and friends who are expecting a certain girl to walk through that door. Seems he's been a little too free with his details about the kind of girl he was fake dating.

"Wait," I stop him. "What's the name of this imaginary woman you've been dating all this time?"

"She doesn't have a name. Just a nickname." I swear he's blushing. "Cookie."

"Cookie?"

"Cookie."

I nod slowly, letting it sink in. "Cookie."

He shrugs. "We were eating chocolate chip cookies with my sister's kids. That was what came to mind."

"Cookie." The more I think about it. The funnier it is. And next thing I know, I'm laughing. "Cookie?"

Now he's laughing. And then we're both laughing. Hard.

Kari's voice calls across the café. "Keep it down over there, kids! Or else Santa is bringing you coal…" She has a playful threat in her voice.

"Just coal?" I squeeze out between giggles. "No cookies?"

And that sets us off again.

When we finally collect ourselves, he tells me more about his family. His mother's chronic illness, his father's doting on his mother, his sister and her family as well as the extended family he sees regularly.

It's pretty picturesque.

"There's a part of me that wants to just come clean with them." His eyes look down, and a sudden sadness comes over him. "But my mom just isn't in a good place right now. I want to let her down easy. So I figure we can do your event on the twenty-second, then dinner at my sister's on the twenty-third. We can call things off between Christmas and New Year's, and they'll be none the wiser. I'll make sure it sounds like we're still going to be friends and that will ease their worries."

I clear my throat. Time to focus on the primary objective here. "Yes, I believe we can make this work."

He stands and walks behind me, lifting my coat and holding it out so I can slip my arms in. "In that case, we will need to do a crash course on each other's likes and dislikes, favorite foods, key life events."

"Don't forget," I wag my finger, "how you take your martini. That *will* come up at the Huxton Christmas."

"That's easy," he lifts an eyebrow and puts on a bad British accent, "shaken, not stirred."

I roll my eyes. "Prepare a one-pager. I'll do the same. Here's my card. I assume we don't need to put this in writing?"

Put this is writing?

He laughs. "No. We're good."

I'm seven minutes late for the team meeting back at Rockin' HQ. Mr. D. gives me the evil eye as I slip into the back. The whole staff is here and the project screen shows a table layout to rival LAX airport.

"Shannon, when you're prepping the servers, remember," he lights a little red pointer onto a table on the screen, "Ms. Zaneth is gluten-free while Ms. Safronay is lactose intolerant. Not so much as a mention or we'll find ourselves with another foie gras incident." Evil eye in my direction again.

"I would have picked foie gras, too," Kieran – who's in

charge of valet service – whispers in my ear. "Who knew what they do to the geese to make them so tasty? Not I."

"Thanks," I mouth and then turn back to the screen. This is my moment. I have to know who is who and, more important, who cannot cross who. I check the diagram against the list in my clipboard. Madame Renaud will be sitting with Miss Chardonnay, that's a good match. Miss Chardonnay owns the Chateau Rose and loves any opportunity to speak French. Madame Renaud refuses to believe that America is not a French colony, so the two should get along just fine.

As for Mr. Needham and the Duke of Headington, that's a different story. I memorize their seats on the map. Four tables apart. That's reasonable until the Duke gets into the wine. This is exactly where my arrangement with Dr. Chamberlain can help. Yes, I could put him on Duke duty.

Dr. Chamberlain. *Tom.* I'd better get used to calling him Tom.

I walk out of that meeting with a to do list longer than I have hours in the day. Four days until the event and I have no idea how I'm going to get it all done.

Cornelius is a ball of excitement when I get home. "A quick walk, okay buddy? There's more snow out there than you like anyway." He doesn't like it when the snow reaches his belly. And for a mini dachshund, that doesn't take much. But he's somehow thrilled to play in the white stuff this evening. Even though I have a ton to do, who can resist playing snowball fetch with a sausage dog while little snowflakes fall?

My phone rings.

"Amelia," I answer without pause, "what am I going to do?"

"Is it about the date?"

"No, it's about designing personalized menus designed on my computer. I cannot get this font right and there are hundreds of them to write up and I have to send them to the printer in the morning and I don't have time to figure it out!"

"Take a breath," her voice brightens, "that's something I can help with. I'll be over in twenty with a pug, a pizza, and my laptop."

Friends. Lifesavers. No need to mention the arrangement with Dr. Chamberlain just yet.

My stomach growls, though I didn't even notice I was hungry.

Hours go by and the menus are sorted. Amelia has passed out on the sofa with Cornelius and Max in her arms. They look so cute. I really hope things work out for Amelia and vet school. It's a massive commitment, but she's got what it takes. Even if she doubts herself sometimes. Who knows, maybe she could even work with Dr. – I mean, Tom.

Just as I think of him, my phone dings with an email.

It's three in the morning.

Subject line: *My one-pager turned four-pager.*

I'm exhausted. I've got meal orders for two hundred picky eaters to confirm. I should sleep…

But I won't.

I curl up in bed and open the attachment, suddenly not caring if I get a wink of sleep at all.

TOM

I tried to sleep. It didn't work.

A one-pager? How does someone sum up every important aspect of their life into a one-pager? I hope that she isn't a stickler for page length, because while I want her to know about me, I also want to know more about her than fits in a page.

That's what I realized as I was lying in bed at four in the morning, hoping her reply would come through and knowing it wouldn't until the morning.

And then my phone buzzes with the familiar vibration of an email arriving.

Is it possible?

The email is short and simple with an attachment. "I guess the point of a one-pager wasn't clear." And then she signs off with a winking emoticon.

If I weren't so tired I'd laugh out loud. "LOL". Hey, I know a thing about modern language.

Just thinking that makes me feel old. But twenty-nine isn't old.

I guess that's part of what happens when we have to grow up fast.

That's what I'd tried to tell her in my letter. That it's important to me not to let my family down because of all they did for me as a kid, the sacrifices they made. The accident I was in when I was seven changed everything. According to physics, I shouldn't have survived. But according to God, I did. It was a miracle that now, as a vet, I know shouldn't have been possible.

But the surgeries, the hospital stays, the ongoing physiotherapy. All that on a teacher and a janitor's salary. My sister, six years older, who didn't move away to study so that she could help with appointments.

That's what took up more than half of my four-page one-pager. Because these people matter to me more than anyone in the world, and I'm dedicated to making sure they don't have to worry about me again.

Getting this job at the Dog's Paw was a dream. I'm still so close to home, and I got to set up the practice from nothing. The place used to be just a dog spa attached to the Chateau Rose, but they were regularly having to call in the city vet due to rich peoples' dogs getting into various mischief like eating curtains or sniffing skunks, that it was worth it to bring someone on the payroll.

Right place at the right time.

That, and a good word from Amelia. Miss Chardonnay loves Amelia, and she'd heard me speak at a college event about vet school. I'd never seen a kid with such bright eyes during a rather dull presentation about internship opportunities. She'll go far.

And who'd have thought she'd be at the center now of this strange-but-perfect situation with Claire?

Claire. What's she doing now?

Rolling over, I smack the light on my alarm clock. Four-twelve in the morning. If she's wise, she's sleeping. With the days we've got ahead of us, I should be doing the same.

Except that I won't.

I open the attachment on her email.

It's one page. But it is the densest one page I think I've ever seen. And that's coming from a med school grad.

Unlike my missive, hers is all factual. And facts, it seems, she's not short of.

Nearly failed out of high school due to an undiagnosed learning disability. Then she had to show them all. (That sounds about right with what I've seen of her so far.)

Studied and worked to pay for school, all the way through to her MBA. (Perseverant, committed, go-get-em attitude, also consistent.)

A line up of bad guys she dated due to a toxic combination of low self-esteem and the misguided belief she could change them. Then she lists them off, including their infractions. While I thought her primary concern was the consumption of tiramisu, her one-pager outlines a series of bad, bad stuff.

He called her *what*? I don't think that word has ever left my lips before.

And that next guy, he stole how much money from her, claiming she owed it to him for a series of random bad fix-it jobs in her apartment? What a douche bag. Wait, can I say douche bag? Is that just another one of my oddball outdated phrases?

Now she has the chance to redeem herself. She's moments away from a big promotion. Everyone at her office is talking about it. But she's got something to prove.

And I have to help her do it.

I'm thinking up all kinds of smart ways to help her shine, to lift her up on that pedestal so that everything she's overcome can be the foundation of her bright future.

The sun rises as I drift off to thoughts of Claire opening champagne, the foam flying all over the place as she celebrates her big promotion. In my daydream, during these last seconds before sleep, she turns to me and mouths, "Thank you."

EIGHT-THIRTY-SEVEN IN THE MORNING AS I SKID TO A STOP IN front of the Dog's Paw. First day *ever* that I'm late.

"Dr. Chamberlain! Oh, thank the mighty lord!"

My first client, Janet Spinx. Yes, *that* Janet Spinx from the 80s fame of "Sing your heart out" and "Don't you know me?" She happens to be a big fan of Corgis. I believe she has twelve of them on her ranch.

And by ranch, I mean a converted tire factory in the center of town which has been done up as a ranch. I only know that from a house call I made during a bad spell of giardia that was passing through her pack.

"I'll be right with you, Ms. Sp–"

"Mind your step! Teacup Yorkies behind you!"

The Dog's Paw is bursting today! I can hardly maneuver my way through.

"This way, class of agility level nine!" Julio screams.

"Get back here!" Nisha cries as a feisty chihuahua runs perpetually one foot in front of her.

"Over here, Prince Gregory!" Amelia calls and the chihuahua runs in her direction, lapping something off her fingertips as she attaches a clasp to his collar. "Peanut butter and ham. Gets him every time."

"I can't bear it–" Nisha takes a growling Prince Gregory in her arms.

"Dr. Chamberlain! Please!" Ms. Spinx holds her corgi in

the air, no small feat given the size of him. "Donovan has a rash across his belly! You must help us!"

"–he's the only dog who wiggles away from my grooming station!" Nisha stomps off as Miss Chardonnay comes in sashaying, because that's what she does instead of walking.

"Ms. Spinx," I say in my doctor-calm voice. It's well-practiced. "I will ring Rita and let you know when I'm ready. We'll get Donovan all sorted out."

I'm not sure how I made it to my clinic wing. My head is pounding. No morning coffee. Does that make me an addict? Oh yeah, I slept for a grand total of one point five hours last night. That would explain the headache.

And I don't regret it for a second.

Until I look in the mirror. I'm pretty sure I aged seven years overnight. A splash of cold water on my mug, and I'm ready for Ms. Spinx. As ready as I'll ever be…

My phone dings.

"Unexpected break at thirteen hours fifteen. Coffee?"

"You bet," I say and she clicks the call off.

Yes. For so many reasons, yes. Also, I didn't know regular people lived using a 24-hour clock, but hey, nothing is 'regular' about Claire.

Between the Yorkies and their *en masse* grooming (no idea how Amelia and Nisha handled that), a last minute class for the Best In Show dogs with Julio, and a series of medical emergencies brought to my wing (only one of which was a true emergency, but thank goodness we treated that spider bite in time), it's nearly quarter to one before I've blinked an eye.

Rita shuffled my appointments around so that "thirteen hours fifteen" is clear. I've just got one more appointment and I'm free as a bird. An easy-going golden called Bella.

"I don't get it," Miss Burke explains. "She's just slowly

become more and more lethargic. Bella even got a bit snippy with me when I tried to talk to her about her weight."

Don't make a face. "Tell me more."

"Just look at her!" Miss Burke cries and then composes herself. "I'm worried for her *health*, not her looks."

"I understand." I don't understood at all. Miss Burke is skinny as a rake. She'd have to be, considering that she's the spokesperson for Slim Me Up milkshakes, though I suspect her gangliness is genetic. Another one of the Chateau Rose's famous clients.

As regards Bella, the issue is plain and clear to me, though Miss Burke seems out of the loop.

I must approach this gently.

Clear throat. Prepare words. Seven minutes before I have to leave for Café Java. "You are aware of Bella's – um – *condition*, right?"

"Condition?" she screeches in a pitch that rivals a fire alarm. "My puppy has a condition?"

I try to smile as reassuringly as I can. "Bella is pregnant."

"Pregnant!" Miss Burke turns to Bella, who, in true Golden Retriever fashion, shrinks under her angry eye. "Pregnant! How *could* you, Bella Burke! Was it the terrier next door? I *told* you to be careful around him and his indiscriminate humping. Oh, this is a nightmare!"

Don't laugh. Don't laugh. For her this is very serious.

I manage to calm Miss Burke and sort out some follow up visits for Bella, who now refuses to come out from under the examination table.

"Can you take care of this?" I whisper to Amelia who conveniently walks by just when I need her. "We can consider this part of an informal veterinary internship."

She purses her lips. "Pregnant golden retriever. Overanxious owner." She nods. "I've got this." She marches into the room and puts a hand on Miss Burke's arm. "You must be so upset. But I've got good news. There's a real market for mama dogs with their litter in the world of publicity and stock photography. Bella could be a model."

Oh, she's good.

"A model?" Miss Burke blows her nose loudly. "My Bella could be a model? Well, I hadn't considered that possibility before."

They are going to be just fine.

CLAIRE

There is absolutely no reason to be nervous. This is the next step in solidifying our business relationship in order to make this holiday season more bearable than those previous.

"Extra cocoa on top today." I nod, knowing Kari will understand.

She sucks in air between her teeth. "Big event coming?"

"You could say that."

The door jingles.

She winks at me. "I think the big event just walked through the door."

Strolling up behind me is Dr. Chamberlain. I mean, Tom. I've got to call him Tom. No one will ever believe he's my boyfriend if I keep calling him doctor. Unless they think it's some kind of weird love game, and that is *not* the impression I'm trying to make!

"Good to see you, Doctor Tom." Doctor Tom? At least that was closer.

"And it's good to see you, Event Promoter Extraordinaire Claire." That gleam in his eye is awfully cheeky. There are girls out there who love that stuff, though I've always gone for more of the quiet, broody type. I wonder how he's still single?

He leans over my shoulder. "What's she having?"

"Double Christmas spice cappuccino with extra cocoa on top." Kari is doing that thing with her tongue in her lip like she knows something the rest of us don't. Note to self, give her a stern warning not to embarrass me in front of my fake boyfriend next time.

Fake boyfriend…

"Make it two." He looks at me. "Who can turn down extra cocoa?"

I decide it's better not to wait until we're at the table. We have limited time to make this happen. "I have a proposal for you," I speak loudly over the hiss of the coffee machine. "We have a rehearsal for the Huxton event tonight, so I thought you could pick me up for a late dinner. That way the staff already have a line of sight on you and there won't be any shock when you appear in two days at the actual event."

"Why does that matter?"

"You don't know my colleagues."

They are bound to make fools of themselves when they meet Tom for the first time. It's much better that it's out of their system before the Huxton dinner. And the sooner, the better, as far as I'm concerned. I'm not looking forward to it. It's bad enough when they do it to a real romantic interest, but with the arrangement the doctor and I have, it's all the worse.

Probably best I don't tell Tom too much about it.

"In that case, you're probably right. Though I have plans."

Plans? I hadn't counted on plans.

"I see. A date?"

"That's exactly right."

Wait, if he's off dating someone else, that risks really

throwing a wrench in our plans. What if someone sees him out with this random chick and then shows up at the Huxton Christmas on my arm? I don't even want to think of the drama!

He takes a loud sip of coffee. "She's a gorgeous brunette, about to give birth to quintuplets."

"What?" I drop my coffee on the table and it splashes up, getting me in the eye. "Ouch!"

"Oh geez, I didn't mean to shock you!" He takes a napkin and dabs at my cheek. "She's a chocolate Labrador and we need to induce tonight for the safety of the pups."

"Well," I take the napkin from his hand and blot at the splotch of brown in the middle of my white chiffon blouse, "I can honestly say I didn't see that coming."

"So I could tell from the look on your face!"

There's a warm feeling growing up the sides of my neck. What is it about this whole situation that has me blushing more in a day than I have in years!

Get ahold of yourself, Claire. This might feel like fun and games, but there is a very real promotion at the end of this if I play my cards right.

And that is a really big 'if'.

"Aha." Tom sits back in his chair. "I can see that we are about to get down to it. I'll put my playful puns aside."

"Why do you say that?"

He points at my cheek. "The corners of your eye change. When you want to talk about something that matters, they lose their crinkle and become firmly set in your cheek. You've done it every time you want to move into a more serious subject."

He can see all of that in the corner of my eyes?

I clear my throat.

"So we're on. Meet me at the Midtown Ballroom as soon as the brunette is in the clear?"

"Perfect."

"Oh yeah, did you read my one pager?" I mean to ask it professionally, but even I hear a note of anxiety in my voice.

"I did."

"No questions?"

"I found it perfectly in keeping with the woman I so far know you to be. Though if we really want to be convincing, then at some point we're going to have to let down more of our guard." He shifts in his chair. "I say that purely from a practical standpoint. My sister and mother lack what I think most people call a filter. Anything is bound to come out of their mouths. And I've already assured them that 'Cookie' is unflappable."

"Unflappable is my middle name. And besides, you're gonna get a run for your money tonight."

"In that case," he crosses his arms like he owns the place, "tonight will be our first test. I'm up for it. Are you?"

"One hundred percent."

He laughs. "We'll see about that."

I LEAN AGAINST THE DOOR OF THE MIDTOWN, WATCHING POOR Tom being fed to the wolves.

"But how did you meeeet?" Silvia whines. Everything that comes out of her mouth is a whine.

This is the part where Tom has to retell the story he sold to his family about how he and "Cookie" met. He gave me the details - met on a boat, Cookie fell into his arms, and the rest was history.

But I'm eager to hear it being told. Tom looks at me before he begins.

"It was on a river cruise. Actually, the cruise was already over, if I'm precise. We were coming off the boat and her heel got wedged in the dock. Fortunately, I was there to catch her."

His recounting is perfect. Factual with a dab of suave.

The wolves lap it up.

"And then what happened?" Lidia, Silvia's identical twin sister is googly-eyed and transfixed. She's always the easiest one to win over.

I had expected the wolves to be more accusatory and suspicious like they've been with my past dates. Instead they are curious and giggly.

And now I'm starting to wonder... He and I never got into this level of detail, he's going to have to invent some extra flair for the story.

"Guess. I'll give you a hint." He raises his eyebrows. "It was in true Claire fashion."

He's loving it. Who could've known the vet has a flair for the dramatic?

"You swept her off her feet, straight to the restaurant for a romantic dinner?"

"No."

Petra raises her hand. "I know! She warned you not to catch random women ever again and you rode off into the sunset!"

"I've seen that movie. Nope."

"I love a mystery," Kieran declares. "But put us out of our misery and tell."

"As you know," he glances at me but I can't read the look in his eyes, "our Claire is first class. She was so grateful not to end up in the water, and so full of admiration in her eyes that as I set her back on her feet... she offered me free graphic design for my next event."

The crowd of twelve howls at my expense.

It's perfect.

"But Claire is so cold." That's Martin with his endearing

Mexican accent. It's a good thing he's such a sweetie, because talk about no filter. He's my buddy and he's my worst headache, all at once. "How did you possibly break through that hard exterior to find the tiny bit of romance inside? No one has emotional walls like her."

Thanks, Martin. How about you just get back to assembling that life-size paper maché boat in the foyer, huh?

Tom is unfazed.

"A woman like Claire is not one you 'break through', Martin. Do you know what she went through to finish her education? I *admire* her. Sure, she has her walls, and every right to them. Don't we all? The best I can do is prove myself worthy and hope that one day she lets me in." He looks at me.

Everyone is silent. He holds my eyes while I try to figure out what's going on in his. Is that the way he really feels? Or is this all part of the masquerade?

He removes himself from the group - who are all still gawking at him - and puts his arm around me.

"It's been great meeting you all. Thank you for the lively chatter. And Wendy, I meant what I said about bringing your pup to the clinic. I might be able to clear that skin irritation up once and for all. Now, I must take care of our leading lady before the big event in forty-eight hours."

He's become the snake charmer of the event planning world.

"You all take care now!" He waves and leads me toward the parking lot.

"See you soon, Doctor Tom!"

"So lovely to meet you!"

"Have fun, you crazy kids. But not too much..." Thanks, Martin.

I toss my stuff into the car. "Where to now?"

He points across the street. "Let's keep it simple and go to 'I Heart Burgers'. What do you say?"

Burgers? Does this guy have any idea what it takes to keep myself in shape while working mad hours and binging on those individually wrapped chocolates?

Then again… I look down at myself. I've lost weight. Not in the good way.

"Burgers sound great."

Once we're settled in and have ordered the 'Double Cheese Tower of (Dis)Grace' for him and the 'Lean Mean Beefy Machine' for me, I feel it's time to circle back to his performance earlier. Encourage his enthusiasm. If he feels appreciated then he's more likely to repeat the behavior, right? That's the philosophy I'm going with, anyhow.

Where have I heard that before?

Oh yeah, dog training.

"You were amazing back there." I mean it.

He waves like he's shy, but I've seen him in action now. I'm not fooled. "It was nothing."

"No really, you were right in character! If I didn't know better, I'd say you really understood me."

He shifts in his chair, looking uncomfortable. "Well, your letter…"

"I loved the way you worked the crowd, leading them on with little invented details. This is precisely the attitude you have to bring to the Huxton event. And then, that last bit, about breaking through my walls? Inspired! Where did you find this material?"

He looks at his hands. Did I go too far? Is the flowing encouragement too much for his humble self?

"Yeah," he finally says. "Just picked up on a vibe, I guess."

"It was great, really." I reach out and put my hand on his. "It means so much to me that you take this seriously."

He's blushing, I can tell. Is it because I'm holding his hand? It's true that I'm finding it a little awkward now, too. I lift my hand and bang the table with a pretend gavel.

"That's it."

He swallows. "That's what?"

"To show you my gratitude, I'm going to offer you free graphic design for your next event."

He laughs, deep and hearty enough to get Cornelius doing his happy bark.

Gotta love a humble, articulate dog lover vet with a big laugh.

I mean, gotta *like* him. Or enjoy his company. Or make the most of this fake relationship while it lasts.

Yeah, that's what I meant.

In order to control this mess of words in my head, I hereby commit to only talking about safe subjects for the rest of the night. His family, my work, and the massive moment of truth known as the Huxton Christmas Extravaganza.

That *is* what this is all about, after all.

TOM

That surgery was a tough one. But when a shepherd's stomach flips, we have precious little time to take action.

Fortunately, Jagger is going to make it. Even though I'm exhausted, there's nothing like the gratitude in the eyes of a pet owner who feared the worst when I get to tell them it's all going to be okay.

I haul myself to the reception desk where Rita is waiting with a cup of steaming peppermint tea for me.

"There you go, doc. And even one of the little cakes I'm trying out for Café Java."

"It's delicious. What's making it spicy?"

"Paprika."

"Paprika, in cake… you're a culinary genius!"

She blows on her nails. "Just doing what a pastry chef must do. And the other good news is that you're done for the day."

I shuffle through my iPad. This move online is a smart one but I'll be darned if I can't figure this thing out. "But there was one more…"

"It was non-essential. I called Ms. Donahue and explained that you had an emergency surgery and she was totally fine to move it to after Christmas. Besides, I believe you have quite an event tonight…"

Can't keep much of a secret around here. I guess The Dog's Paw isn't so different from the Rockstar Event Promotions crowd. But at least no one here grills me on the details.

They just make assumptions and whisper rumors. Hmmm.

"Who told you that?" I sip the warm goodness of peppermint healing.

"Oh please," Rita stands up, "you're the one who's mentioned it three times so far today."

I choke on my tea. "I did?"

Rita pushes the wheely chair away and saunters toward my clinic. "I'll clean up your office today. An early Christmas gift. More time for you to primp and preen." She winks and is gone, leaving me with my mouth gaping open.

I suppose it *has* been on my mind. And I *have* been looking forward to it. But not because of the event, and not even because I'll finally be able to put this charade with my family to rest.

But because every minute I'm with Claire, I feel like a better man.

I'm sure it's just because she gives me so much attention. I'm not used to it. It's nice to be encouraged, supported, and she tries to understand me. There's nothing unusual about that. It could be any girl - I mean, woman - showing me attention. It would have the same effect.

Right?

No, it totally wouldn't.

Who am I kidding? What am I going to do with this schoolboy crush on the fake girlfriend I have to dump in a week?

I barely get into the car in a daze when my phone rings.

I try to answer it on this fancy Bluetooth in my car, but I can't get it to work.

"Tom? Tom? Are you there?" My sister's timing is always awesome. And by awesome, I mean awful.

"I'm here, hang on, I'm trying to-"

"Are you in the car? You have to put me on Bluetooth."

Her voice is still coming out of the tiniest speaker known to man at the bottom of my phone. "I know, hang on. I can't connect…"

"Did you set it up the way I told you? Auto-connection on discovery?"

"I thought so…"

I can hear Jen sigh from miles away. "You're hopeless."

Suddenly the car talks to me. *"Connecting."*

"Jen? Are you there?"

"YES, I'M STILL HERE. CAN YOU HEAR ME NOW?"

I can't turn down the volume fast enough.

"Yes, I can."

"For a guy who went to Med school, you're pretty hopeless on technology."

"Thanks, sis. I'll have you know I saved a young German Shepherd this afternoon." Jen has a soft spot for German Shepherds, insisting on calling them by their European name of *Alsatian*.

"Aw, you saved an Alsatian? Well done, little bro. You do us all proud. Speaking of proud, are you still bringing your pride and joy tomorrow?"

I smile at the thought of Claire gliding into dinner with the family. They won't know what hit them. "Sure am."

"Finally, we get to meet Cookie! I was half-sure you were going to drop a bomb and tell us she couldn't make it after all."

"She'll be there. She can't wait. But that said, I've got to help her tonight with work, so I've really got to go."

"Tom, are you still there. TOM?"

"I'm here, I'm here, no need to shout." I turn down the volume a little further.

"You know how much this means to Mom, right?"

"I do."

"Good kid."

"I'm taller than you, sis."

"Tell Cookie we're thrilled, and go have fun tonight."

"Thanks-"

"And Tom?"

"Yeah?"

"DON'T MESS THIS UP!"

"*Disconnected*," the car tells me.

Don't mess this up. Wise advice, sage sister. If only you knew how much I've already messed everything up. First in creating this mirage of a romance to fool you and mom, and now by creating a mirage with a woman I just might be falling for.

Stop it, Tom. You're an adult. This is infatuation. You're out of practice, that's all.

I look into the rear view mirror. "She doesn't see you as anything except a temporary arrangement, so you'd better get that into your head." I point at the dufus in mirror. "So follow your sister's advice and don't mess - AHHHH!"

Rita is banging on the window and just about giving me a heart attack. I roll down the window.

"Did I forget something?"

"You've been sitting here talking to yourself for the last ten minutes. Get moving!"

"I was talking to my sister on Bluetooth, I'll have you know."

"Bluetooth? You?" She cocks her head and then waves her

hand. "I don't believe it. Go home and shower before the big event. You smell like a wet dog!"

MY PHONE DINGS AS I STEP OUT OF THE SHOWER. CAREFUL not to drip on the home button - I've made that mistake before - I see the text from Claire.

"Café knot your tie if you can. That's all the rage and the Duke of Headington is bound to comment on it positively."

Café knot the tie. I haven't worn a tie since I graduated from vet school, only had one in my drawer for funerals which thankfully I haven't had to use. When Claire heard that she had one overnight shipped from a fancy store in New York.

Glad it wasn't the tie that threw this evening off.

I search how to do this mystical café knot, and indeed it is all the rage among a certain elite. I'm guessing they have personal assistants or something to help them with it, because my two hands are sorely insufficient to make it work.

Check the clock, twenty-two minutes before I pick up Claire. She did all the set up and had fifty-seven minutes to get home, change, and get back to the Midtown. It seemed only natural I would pick her up, but the look of surprise on her face when I'd suggested it told me she hadn't assumed anything.

That would be wonderful, she'd said, as if it weren't the most normal thing in the world. I guess that's what happens where you get so used to doing everything yourself. Small acts make a big difference.

I check myself out in the mirror. Not bad, Dr. Chamberlain. That trim of the beard has done wonders for replacing "rugged" with "dapper". As for the tie… I think this is what it's supposed to look like.

I have a funny feeling someone is watching me. Yes, through the window, the neighbor's Calico cat.

"I can feel you judging me from here."

The cat doesn't react.

I do a little runway walk. "See? This is what it's supposed to look like." I finish with a spin and knock my knee into the toilet. "Ouch."

The cat blinks once to show its indifference.

"I'm gonna go now. You can sit there all night telling me I'm a dork, but there's a girl waiting for me to pick her up."

Another blink and then the cat takes off, as cats are wont to do.

"Mr. Needham, owner of seventeen insurance companies." I remind myself on the drive over. Claire was clear. Names and responsibilities matter, as well as small details that I can bring up casually in conversation. "Loves golf, won a tournament once in Japan. Don't talk about citrus fruits." She didn't tell me why. What's the guy got against citrus fruits?

The roads are slick with the layer of slow that has melted and is now refreezing. Nights like this make me grateful for winter tires. Working way out at the Dog's Paw, I wouldn't have it any other way. Those country highways can be treacherous.

I swing in front of Claire's building where she's waiting for me in a full length navy woolen coat. Her white gloves catch the moonlight as she waves and something in her hair sparkles like she's a holiday angel.

What is it about little details women do that turn men into blithering idiots?

I will not let her tremendous beauty derail me. Tonight I

am on my game, ready to play the role and live up to the promise of the most charming of escorts.

Yikes, that sounds bad. Chaperone? No, she's not twelve.

"Hi," she says, slipping into the seat. "I'm in, you can drive now. I have twelve minutes before check in time."

"What do I call myself to you?"

"Stick with Tom." There's no hint of humor in her tone. I should get the car moving, and I do. She sighs, I can hear her relaxing.

But I need to know the right term. "I mean, I'm not your chaperone."

"Of course you're not. I'm not twelve."

"That's what I thought. So then, what am I?"

"Tonight, you're my boyfriend."

"Boyfriend. Got it." I will not let myself believe it. I will not let myself believe it. I will not...

"But just call yourself Tom. That's best."

We swing into the parking lot with ninety seconds to spare.

"It's slippery! I am not wearing the right footwear for this!"

She looks like a baby deer wobbling its first steps. In that second, I can see where this is heading, starting with a sudden fall, followed by a trek to the emergency room, and topping it off with a cast for Christmas.

I can't let that happen. I'm her boyfriend tonight, after all.

"Hang on, I gotcha."

I rush over and lift her into my arms. She's a heck of a lot easier to maneuver than that German Shepherd. Who knew lifting humans was so simple?

Her arms around my neck, I can feel her breath against my cheek. The fog from her lips makes little clouds over our heads.

She whispers, sending chills down my spine. "Seems your grip is better than mine."

"I never understood impractical footwear."

"It's what women do to look good to the rest of the world."

"Pfft. I think you'd look great in overalls and sneakers."

I set her down on the cleared front step of the Midtown, finally able to see the demure smile across her face. "Thanks, Tom." Her brow then furrows. "What on earth have you done to your tie?"

I try to look down, but it's tied so tightly around my neck that I can't lower my head.

"It's that café knot you told me about."

"Oh, Tom." She reaches up and unwinds the mass of necktie under my chin. Her fingers then navigate adeptly, and whatever she's done, it's a heck of a lot more comfortable and no longer cuts off my windpipe. "It's like this."

"Much better." I don't want her to let go. I want her to keep a hold of me all night. But she steps back and admires her work, just as I notice something awfully strange in the lobby. "Is that Santa's head? You decapitated Santa for your party?"

"And we'll soon set it on fire. All the rage this year…"

I never did understand popular culture.

"Claire! Claire!" A man's raspy voice booms throughout the lobby.

"Coming, Mr. Denudo." She takes my arm and leads me (which makes it look like I'm leading her, which I find impressive) to the other side of the lobby where a grand entrance has been done up with twinkling lights and silver snowflakes. "Let me introduce you to Tom."

"Tom." He extends his hand. "Gerard Denudo. My friends call me Gerry, but you're not my friend yet, got that?"

I take his hand and shake it firmly. "Yes, sir."

Claire gasps. "Mr. Denudo-"

"I'm just kidding! It's Christmas. Can't an old guy make a joke at Christmas? Call me Gerry."

Claire shakes her head. "Sir, I can see you're in a good mood, but let me remind you that the Huxton Christmas event..."

"Yeah, yeah. Don't you worry about a thing. I'm going to be all business once the clients filter in. I don't need a repeat of 1976." He spins on his heel and heads inside the main hall.

"What happened in 1976?" I quietly ask Claire.

"None of us know, but it involved the President of the United States, and it was bad. Come, I need to do the staff check-in and then our work really begins."

Claire sets me down at a table with a warning not to touch the dessert bar. The band warms up, and I wonder if I'm going to suffer under Christmas crooning all night.

Kieran, whom I met the other night, stops by my table.

"Tom, good to see you. Claire sent me. You're to 'work the lobby' until the opening ceremony."

"Work the lobby?"

"That's what she said. I've got to go support the valet service now, but catch ya later, bud."

Work the lobby. I don't remember this being in my job description, but if that's what a boyfriend does, then that's what a boyfriend does. Now to remember all the rules Claire laid out. The Duke of Headington cannot be in the same room as Mr. Needham, no way, no how.

Cardinal rule number one: do my best to charm Mrs. Offenstein, who I should be able to pick out of the crowd as she only wears leather and carries her miniature pinscher in a purse. That should make for easy conversation.

People start strolling in.

"Hello," I say to a man who's just come through the door. "Welcome to the Huxton Christmas."

"Ah," the old man says. "Are you the help? I'd like a dry martini, two olives."

"You must be Mr. Jacobs. I've heard a lot about you."

"You have?" He looks suspicious. Oh yeah. He thinks I'm a server.

"In fact, I'm a guest here tonight, and my - uh - date, Claire, has told me much about you."

"I see! You're *Claire's* date. She chewed you up yet?" He laughs with such reckless abandon that I'm almost worried he might have a heart attack. "That girl. She planned my granddaughter's wedding, and it was perfect. But she's sure a handful!"

This is not the conversation I thought I'd be having.

"She and I have lively conversation."

"I'll bet!" And he's off again, giggling more like a teenager than an octogenarian.

"How about I sort out that martini for you, Mr. Jacobs."

"Never you mind that martini, go find your girl and bring her to me for a hello."

Find my girl. Easier said than done. The hall is filling up and I can barely keep track of my own two feet. I'm guessing that stomping all over the guests would put me on the list with the guy who ate too much dessert.

I weave my way through, catching sight of an unusually sized purse in front of me. "I bet that's Winky in there."

The woman, nearly six feet tall in her stiletto heels (seriously, how do women not tip over in those things?) has her white hair pulled back in a tight bun. She looks down her long pointed nose at me, and I can't help but see the family resemblance between her and the dog's head peeking out of the handbag.

"Who's ahhhhhsking?" She drawls with an accent I don't recognize.

"Excuse me for barging in, but I have heard stories of Winky and I happen to be a fan of miniature pinschers."

"Is that riiiiiiight? And what makes a man a fan of any such beast?"

"I'm a vet, ma'am."

"Oh!" Her face completely changes. Her eyebrows lift and the corners of her mouth turn upward. "Please, I must ahhh-hhsk you. Look at Winky's teeth, I beg you. For I am convinced that you shall see a creature more evolved than the others of his species."

I approach Winky carefully. Inspecting a dog in a handbag is not the same thing as at my clinic. But Mrs. Offenstein was one of the people on Claire's list. Anything I can do to make her happy will help the cause.

Winky eyes me suspiciously.

"Don't mind his protests. He's a good boy. He won't bite unless you deserve it."

Looking into his mouth at a fancy Christmas party just might be enough to deserve it. We avoided the emergency room once tonight, I don't want to be the one needing stitches on my thumb. I already got them twice during my early days when I was too cocky with a chihuahua.

"Hi there, Winky," I say in a high pitched voice.

"Why do you talk to him so straaaaange?"

"Just doing my job, ma'am." I turn back to the dog. "Can I have a little look at your toothie-wootsies?"

"Good heavens."

But it worked. Winky is furiously wagging his tail and I can get my pinkie finger into his gums. "That's a good boy."

Sure enough, Winky has two extra little teeth. Is he more biologically advanced? I'm guessing it's more likely a genetic anomaly. But it's Christmas.

"Winky certainly does have something special happening in his mouth."

"I knew it! I knew it! He will go down in hiiiiistory! But what is a vet doing at the Huxton Christmas?"

I look up. Claire has just come on stage with Mr. Denudo. And she's so stunning that I can't speak.

The stage light hits and makes her look like an angel. She's in serious conversation until Mr. Denudo moves toward the microphone. She looks up, meets my eyes, and smiles.

"I'm with her," I manage to say to Mrs. Offenstein.

"Claire? You're with Claire? She planned my seventieth birthday extravaganza. I've never been a fan of her taste in men. Until now."

I think Mrs. Offenstein is still speaking to me, but all I can see is Claire. It's like every light in the world has dimmed except for the one on her, making her glow like the North Star.

I'd better not be rude. "What was that, Mrs. Offenstein?"

"Indeed," Mrs. Offenstein says with a cheeky grin. "I said you appear most smitten. Anyone can recognize puppy love from across a crowded room."

"Me?"

I'm just faking it. I'm faking it. I've got this weird feeling all over, warm like hot cocoa.

I'm faking it.

"Welcome, esteemed guests, fine residents and visiting friends. Welcome to the Huxton Christmas Ball!"

Cheers erupt throughout the room, the three hundred guests appreciating what has become a mainstay of Christmas at Hampton Falls. Most of these guests have been coming for years, some even since the start three decades ago.

The last stragglers get to their assigned seats. I wonder if Tom happened upon Mrs. Offenstein by accident, or if he saw that I'd seated them together. I know many of the guests find Mrs. Offenstein insufferable with her passion for small dogs, but that's exactly what makes Tom a perfect table mate for her.

Mr. Denudo continues. "As we do every year, there will be music!" Cheers from the audience. "There will be dancing!" More cheers. "And there will be a glorious steak dinner crafted by Jean-Philippe Rousseau, direct from France!" More cheers and this time I catch sight of Miss Chardonnay.

"From France?" she declares. "But zees is so unexpected!"

Miss Chardonnay, ironically, comes from the Bordeaux region of France. Everything at the Chateau Rose Hotel is as French as America can get. It's the most luxurious getaway on this side of the Rockies.

Mr. Denudo raises his hands to quiet the crowd. "Before we begin, we must first give warm thanks to our host, and one of this town's oldest families, Mr. James Huxton and his four sons, Douglas, Henry, Louie, and Charles!"

The table of men stand and wave from their place at the front of the room. Four of Hampton Fall's most eligible bachelors, and yet they evade all signs of settling down. It makes me think of what Tom said about the line men give about not being ready for commitment.

Tom. I hope he's okay down there. With the lights in my eyes, it's hard to read the crowd, much less make out the details of their faces. I'm looking forward to getting off this stage. I'm doing my duty, like I've done every year for the past four years. Standing behind Mr. D. to offer whatever support he may need. Once he broke out in hives while in the middle of his goodnight speech, but I was standing by with a first aid kit, complete with antihistamine. He's had me on stage with him ever since.

"This year," Mr. Denudo goes on, "I want to bring someone into the light who is normally hiding behind it. You all know her well, and this year she is the one who took the reins to lead on this entire Christmas ball!"

Oh no. He's setting me up so that if people hate it, then they know exactly who to blame.

"Many of you know her well, she has designed your weddings, your birthdays, your retirement parties. She has grown up in front of our eyes. I give you… Claire Ingram!"

A spotlight lands on me. I've got do something classy, they're all clapping, I can't just wave.

I curtsy.

Heaven help me, I just curtsied in heels and a velvet cocktail dress. Somebody chuckled, I heard it.

The light flickers back to Mr. Denudo as I remain blinded in the aftermath of the spotlight directly in the eye. I just have to get off this stage. Mr. D. is giving his final words.

"Eat, drink, be merry, one and all!"

Everyone cheers and the band strikes up again, Mr. Denudo taking the lead guitar for a few songs. Couples make their way to the dance floor as it's one of those classic rock Christmas songs they all love.

You can take the rockstar off the stage, but he's still going to rock out any chance he gets.

I slither to the back of the stage where I can finally get the lay of the land. Mrs. Offenstein is off-her-chair happy. I've never seen her smile like that! What did Tom do to cheer up that sourpuss? Over there is Mr. Needham, minding his business, and that's just as well. Two years ago nearly had us end the event early - never before done in the thirty years of Huxton Christmas Balls.

Oh no. The Duke of Headington, and he's heading that way - straight for Mr. Needham! I can't possibly get off the stage fast enough to prevent it from happening. Think fast, what can I do? Create a scene? Scream and faint? No, that's not any better. Where's the fuse box? If only I could turn off all the lights I might be able to distract them. I have no clue where the fuse box is and there's barely fifteen feet between them now!

Wait, is that?...

Tom.

He extends his hand to the Duke, and seems to be making some kind of compliment that the Duke brushes off, though I'm sure he's actually soaking it up. Tom insists and the Duke puts a hand on Tom's shoulder. He points at the tie. I knew it. I knew the café knot was going to be a winner!

Tom and the Duke head back in the opposite direction toward the lobby.

Saved.

The first twenty minutes have gone brilliantly. Only another three hours and forty minutes to go.

I can mingle among the crowd for a few minutes. The first course will be ready in ten, just enough time to show my face and apologize in advance for any unwanted drama.

"Claire! Yoohoo Claire!" I'd recognize that French accent anywhere.

"Hello Miss Chardonnay, are you having a lovely evening?"

"It was dull as ze Picardy region of France in February until I heard that you are the one responsible for the evening's festivities."

I have no idea how to respond to that.

"Allow me to translate." Tom appears behind me. "Miss Chardonnay means that her expectations were low and now she's excited to see what comes next."

"Zis is exactly what I mean."

"In that case, thank you, Miss Chardonnay. I hope we live up to your expectations. I'm sure Jean-Philippe's cuisine will fulfil your gastronomic wishes."

"I have no doubt of eet. I love ze *entrecôte.*"

"Gastronomic wishes?" Tom whispers to me.

"It's a French thing. Let's sit down, the first course is coming."

Several people stop us on our way to the table.

"Your first big event," Mrs. Engles grasps my arm. "I'd better see gluten free on my table."

"Sure is, Mrs. Engles."

The woman beside her screeches, "And you do remember-"

"Lactose intolerant, no cream in your peppercorn sauce, Miss Terren."

The crowd is thick, everyone making their way back to their seats. I didn't realize it, but Tom has taken my hand, leading me forward.

We reach the table and Mrs. Offenstein stands. She leans over, Winky's handbag knocking into my arm. "He's a good catch," she says, lifting her chin in Tom's direction. "So glad you've finally made a smart decision. We've all been worried about you."

She re-takes her seat, effectively ending the conversation.

We've all been worried about you.

Who? Why? Focus, Claire. The first course is being served. Have they laid the fish knives? Yes. The lemon slices? Ah, Jean-Philippe splayed them over the whitefish. Well played, Jean-Philippe. I'd tell him that was a good idea but he knows it already. No one hires Jean-Philippe Rousseau for his humility.

First course goes down without a hitch. I catch Silvia's eye and nod my approval. But she doesn't look relieved, she looks panicked.

"I'll be back," I say quickly to Tom and walk as fast as I can without looking like I'm rushing across the ballroom. I'd run if I could, even in these heels.

I can't get to her fast enough. "What's going on?"

She's pale. "Jean-Philippe said we are not to go into the second kitchen for anything, but we can't plate the main course without him, and the steaks aren't out yet!"

One Frenchman's wrath versus three hundred hungry guests...

I look around the ballroom. People are chatting away, the first course only just now being cleared. I check my watch.

"We're still on course, perhaps it just needed longer to cook than planned?"

"You don't know Jean-Philippe. Everything is planned. This, however, is off-plan."

I don't want to make a scene with Jean-Philippe. That's the sort of thing that could ruin me for this promotion. Mr. D. would tell me I'm not ready, that I still haven't mastered the 'great art of event management'. I can hear his voice already.

"We wait," I tell her, but I can see she's still anxious. "This is on me. Let's give him another ten minutes."

A commotion erupts on the far side of the ballroom.

"Winky! Winky! Come back!"

Oh no. This is exactly what I don't need. A mini pinscher running around loose, biting at the guests and soiling the premises.

I make my way back to that side as Tom accompanies Mrs. Offenstein.

"This is so out of character," she's saying as I reach them in the middle of the room. "He's always at my side, always."

"We've got to find him, Tom. He could ruin us!"

Tom thinks for a moment, but I really wish he'd do it faster.

"Mrs. Offenstein, you're certain he wouldn't just run off because he smelled something good or needed a bio break?"

"Never!"

"In that case, something *is* wrong."

Tom walks past me, almost like I don't even exist anymore. He's on a mission, but I have no idea what for. I run to catch up with him.

"Tom! What can I do, how can I help?"

"Do you hear that?" he calls back to me.

"Hear what?"

"Puppy whining."

"I hear the band and I hear three hundred hungry people but no, I don't hear any puppy whining."

He continues on, marching into the kitchen, past Silvia.

"Did a dog come through here?"

"He did. He just tore through, heading for the second kitchen."

"Where is it?" Tom's eyes are wide now, but I wish I knew what was going through his head. This seems crazy, but if he catches the dog, that's all that matters now.

Silvia points and we head there.

"Look!" Tom points at the door to the second kitchen which has a six-inch gap at the bottom of it.

And there's smoke coming out of it.

"Come on!"

Tom rushes in and I'm right on his heels, where Jean-Philippe is collapsed on the floor with Winky licking at his cheek. He's just beginning to rouse when Tom reaches him.

"Chef Jean-Philippe! Can you hear me?"

"Mmmmm," the Michelin chef replies.

I look for the source of the fire and I find it in the industrial oven. I switch the emergency lever and open the front of the oven.

"He's going to be all right," Tom calls over. "Low blood pressure, I think."

"I'm glad to hear he's okay. As for our steaks..."

"Let me see what I can do," Silvia rushes in. "You go work the crowd. My team will salvage what we can."

"WINKY!" Mrs. Offenstein screams from the door! "MY WINKY!"

Winky gives Jean-Philippe's hand a final lick, confident that Tom has the situation covered. Mrs. Offenstein leans over with her handbag open as Winky leaps back into it.

"Let's go tell the guests about the change in dinner plans," Tom leads me out.

But what can I possibly say? This is it. My promotion is

ruined, the night is ruined. The Huxton's might even use one of the event planners just opening up in town. Everything is ruined.

"I can't." I look at Tom and do everything to stop these tears from falling.

"You've got this," he says, putting his hands on my shoulders. "Events are nothing without crisis management. So go manage this crisis, just like you know how."

I manage to nod before climbing up onto the stage. On seeing me, the band fades the music to silent.

I tap the microphone. It's on. I clear my throat.

Everybody is looking at me.

"Hello. Hello, everyone. I'm afraid I have some news. There was a crisis in the kitchen which has affected parts of our dinner, so there will be a delay and change of menu."

I hear them murmuring. I know what they are saying. A disaster. A disappointment. A failure.

"I want to assure you that we will do our best to make up for this setback, and I beg you to accept my apologies-"

"DON'T YOU APOLOGIZE FOR ANYTHING!"

Everyone shifts in their chairs to see where the noise came from.

Mrs. Offenstein.

"Don't you apologize, not for a second. Hang on. I am comiiiiiing up there."

Grumbles emerge from across the crowd and I'm stupefied into silence. She climbs up the front stairs to the stage and nods at me.

"I will take this." She pulls the microphone out of its stand. "Everyone, everyone. Neighbors, friends, and some-times-enemies." Chuckles from a few places in the room. "This young woman and her fine young friend have just saved the life of our chef, Jean-Philippe Rousseau!" Gasps. "If it weren't for them seeking out my Winky, already an admirable task, they found our chef... fainted over the stove!" More gasps. Her facts aren't quite right, but it doesn't seem like the right time to correct her. "And so, dear guests, we cannot let her apologize. If the meal is ruined, then I, for one, applaud their efforts and will go without! To Claire and her fabulous boyfriend, Tom!"

Applause deafen the room, and it goes on for longer than I can count. There are smiles on every face I see, and some start to stand.

Mr. Denudo climbs up on stage and takes the mic, escorting Mrs. Offenstein back to the floor.

"Ladies and gentlemen, you've heard it! Let's hear from the woman of the hour, our Claire!"

Now what?

"Thank you so much for your understanding. But I can't take the credit. Tom is the one who was wise enough to know that we had to find the dog. If it weren't for Tom, who knows what might have happened to Chef Jean-Philippe!"

Mr. Denudo takes the mic. "Tom! Come up here, Tom! Let us appreciate you in true Huxton Christmas fashion!"

Tom jogs through the tables, getting pats on the back on his way. He hops the stairs two by two and takes the mic offered to him by Mr. Denudo.

"Thank you so much for understanding, and I have good news from the kitchen! Dinner is saved! But your steaks will all be 'well done'." The crowd laughs and Tom gives me a wink.

"Finally, I cannot take the credit for having found Jean-Philippe, there's someone else worthy of our admiration. Everybody lift your glasses..."

Champagne is poured across the ballroom, and someone brings us glasses on stage.

"That's right," Tom continues, giving me a smile that melts me from head to toe before he looks out over the crowd. "Lift your glasses… to Winky!"

"TO WINKY!"

TOM

From what I can tell, the rest of the night has gone off without a hitch. More than that, it's like the whole crisis changed the atmosphere. When we got here, things were stuffy. There were all these rules, spoken and unspoken, of who could talk to who, where things should be placed, how to behave.

What I see now is a room full of humanity.

Claire joins me at the dessert table. "Did you see that?"

"Mr. Needham and the Duke shaking hands? Yes, I did."

"I never in a million years could have guessed…"

"That's the Christmas spirit."

She looks up at me. "It's magic."

I swear all I did was blink, but her lips are on mine and now I'm the one who believes in magic.

She takes a step back, a shy smile quickly dances across her face.

"Sorry, it was the moment."

"Please don't apolog…"

"Claire!"

I can't finish the words before Mr. Denudo is in front of us. The spell is broken.

"Claire," Mr. Denudo puts a hand on her shoulder. "Incredible crisis management. Way to go. That's what this business is all about. When the chaos of Christmas passes, we've got to talk. My office, three p.m. on the twenty-ninth. Got it?"

Her eyes are wide like the Christmas ornaments hanging on the wall behind her. "Yes, sir!"

He claps her shoulder and then points at me. "As for you, well done. The two of you make a heck of a match."

He walks away and all I can think is…

We sure do.

"I'll catch you when everyone's gone, okay?" She's on cloud nine, I can see it. "I've got to sort out the breakdown and then my job here will be done. You still good to drive me home?"

"Yes, of course."

She blinks and I'm not sure what she's thinking. "If you need to go earlier, it's no big deal."

"I don't have any other plans."

She nods. "All right then. I really appreciate your efforts so far. I'll see you in about-" she looks at her watch, "-forty-seven minutes."

"That's very precise for about…" I don't finish the thought. She's already gone.

When the forty-seven minutes are up, I pull the car around. No more slip-sliding dramatics tonight.

She hops in, her hair a little messier but more relaxed than I've seen her since this whole thing began.

"You look relieved."

"You have no idea." She pulls the lever and extends the seat to lie all the way down. "I can't believe it, it's done! And even better, people loved it!"

"They sure did."

"And a lot that is thanks to you."

I put the car in gear. "Naw. Just doing my job."

"But you did it very well. The way you charmed the guests, the way you made them believe we were really together…" She pulls the seat back up. "They'll be so disappointed when we break up our fake romance. I think we have some real fans out there!"

I have to watch my words. This isn't the moment. What was that kiss? She was just excited, caught up in the emotion. It didn't have anything to do with us.

Or did it?

Her lips were so soft, and it didn't feel like a "yay everything worked out kind of kiss". But then again, what do I know about types of kisses?

"A penny for your thoughts?"

Thank goodness it's almost midnight so she can't see how red my face is. "Just thinking about dinner tomorrow."

"Of course! I owe you, I really do. And I promise I'll do everything to put on as good a show tomorrow as you did tonight."

"Yeah." Say something. Don't let her hear the disappointment. "That will be swell."

"*Swell?*" She bursts out laughing, the laugh that is a year of stress exploding at once into joyful Christmas spirit. "Where *do* you get this stuff?"

I kissed him.

I kissed him not because he was my fake boyfriend.

Maybe I *should* have kissed him because he was my fake boyfriend.

I kissed him because he's the boyfriend I've always wished for.

But he's a *fake* boyfriend.

Even so, I kissed him. And I meant it.

This loop of thoughts won't let me sleep. How many hours have I been tossing and turning, the same words circling in my head again and again?

I should be the happiest I've ever been. We saved Jean-Philippe. We found Winky. We transformed the snootiest Christmas event into a holiday paradise of goodwill and love. That promotion is all but in the bag.

Isn't that what this was all about, the promotion?

So why do I feel like I'm missing something…something big…

I SWEAR I ONLY JUST SHUT MY EYES AND NOW IT'S ALMOST noon. I suppose that's what months of stress all packed on top of each other will do to a girl.

I roll over and look at my phone. Seven unread messages.

Amelia: *So? How did it go? Max and Cornelius have had a heck of a night with the stuffed reindeer.*

Amelia: *Well?*

Amelia: *Did he do like you told him to? You know, he's one of the good ones.*

Amelia: *Why aren't u replying, are you sick or avoiding me? You can't be sleeping, it's past ten.*

Tom: *Looking forward to tonight. Bring nothing but yourself. I hope th*

Tom: *Sorry, hit send too fast. I hope that you are able to relax now that the Huxton shindig has passed. I hope I lived up to your expectations. I hop*

That is the end of his message. Not sure where he was going to go with that last "I hop" but I assume it was "hope" and not that he was channeling his inner rabbit.

Amelia: *Ahhh, I bet ur sleeping now that yesterday is all finished up. I'll come by with Cornelius in an hour. Sweet dreams, sleeping beauty.*

She sent that one a little over an hour ago, according to the clock.

And there goes the doorbell. I'm sure Amelia won't mind if I answer in my housecoat.

"Whoa!" she says as I pull the door open. "Did you sleep at all?"

Two puppies rush by under my feet, one I assume is Cornelius but I'm moving too slow to catch sight of them before they reach the water bowl in the kitchen.

"Do I look that rough?" I ask Amelia, though all it takes is a glance in the front hall mirror to see that I am somewhere between a zombie (mouth hanging open and all), a raccoon (did I not remove my mascara last night?), and a plain old mess of a girl. "Hmm. I'm going to need to shower before tonight."

"Ah yes," Amelia nods knowingly, "now it's your turn to return the favor."

I zombie my way to the kitchen where the coffee that was automatically made at eight in the morning is still awaiting me. Three spoonfuls of sugar and a minute in the microwave later, I join Amelia on the sofa. And by join, I mean flop my shell of a body onto the cushions.

Bad idea with hot coffee.

"Yikes!" My scalded hands tingles.

"Give me that," Amelia takes the coffee, "and go run your hand under cold water. You are a proper mess today!"

How can I tell her that I was dreaming all night, awake and asleep, about the man who's my fake boyfriend? The whole point of fake is that it isn't real. I should have been able to hit this promotion, shake his hand and move on. But there was something in his eyes yesterday. The genuine pleasure he took in seeing my dreams come true. And never mind that he's practically Superman, saving Jean-Philippe and my reputation all in a single swoop.

But it's not just that, I think as the cold water soothes my throbbing hand. Tom is real. He's himself, and confident about it.

I've spent years running around trying to prove myself. Maybe I've got something to learn from him. At the Huxton Ball, he was a total fish out of water, and that didn't change him in the slightest. He remained, as ever, kind and polite and sweet and funny…

Well, crap. I'm falling for my fake boyfriend.

And worse, tonight I have to fake it in front of his family.

At least the swoony eyes should come naturally enough. Assuming I wash the mascara from underneath them first.

"Come on, spill the beans." Amelia is cross-legged on the floor with the two pups tugging at the stuffed reindeer like it's going out of style.

"You know… it's no big deal."

Amelia gives me *the look*. Any girl who has a best girlfriend who can see right through her knows *the look*.

"Okay then…" I tell her. I tell her everything. *Everything.* Because if you can't tell your best girlfriend about your supercrush on your fake boyfriend, then who can you tell?

"Ah, Clairibell." She shakes her head. "You know that Tom is a confirmed bachelor, right?"

"Meaning?"

"Meaning that he's had women as rich as Lorna van der Camp and women as famous as Trisha Thomas throw themselves at him. He might enjoy their company for a bit, but then they fade into the background, because that's the kind of guy Tom is. That's also why I thought he'd be your perfect fake date. Because a - he likes you and b - he'd never get involved." She sighs. "And you, my beloved bestie, made it very clear that you wanted nothing to do with a man until you made your promotion."

She's right. I swallow hard.

But I'd never expected a man like Tom to rush in and flip my heart upside down.

"It's just a crush." I say it out loud to convince myself as much as to convince Amelia.

"I get it," she says, her eyes sympathetic because I know she does. "I won't even give a guy a second look until I get that admission letter to vet school. We are women with dreams and goals and plans. But a man like Tom is one in a million. Still, Clairibell…" she puts her arm around my shoulders just in time as I can feel unwanted tears building up, "protect your heart."

Protect my heart. I've got to go pretend to be in a relationship in front of the family of the man I have these - unwanted - feelings for, and I've got to protect my heart.

Easier said than done.

Max and Cornelius are rolling over her legs in a battle of the fittest, but even that can't cheer me up.

She gives a sympathetic smile. "You gonna be okay tonight?"

I sigh. "Just call me Cookie."

WHAT'S A GIRL TO WEAR TO MEET THE FAMILY OF HER FAKE boyfriend? I went with black tights and a red velvet cocktail dress. Hopefully it's dressy enough to impress without going over the top. It never occurred to me that I should ask about dress code.

Ding, dong goes the doorbell in that classic way that tells you this is a home where family live. I can hear little feet rushing for the door.

"My turn to open!"

"You opened for Grandma!"

The door creaks open and two little humans, barely tall enough to reach the doorknob are waiting on the other side.

"Hi, I'm C...Cookie."

Cookie. Dang it, Tom, you couldn't come up with something better than Cookie? What about Sweetie Pie, or Snickers, or... never mind. I guess Cookie is just fine.

The kids are looking at me with their mouths hanging open.

"May I come in?" I venture.

The little boy whispers to the little girl, "Is she an angel?"

The little girl nods slowly, staring at me the whole time.

"You two are so sweet, but it's really quite cold out here."

"Are you here for Uncle Tom?" the boy asks with wide

eyes.

"I am."

Tom appears down the hall. "Are you guys going to let Cl…Cookie in or not?"

At least I'm not the only one struggling with my new identity.

He rushes to the door and puts his arm around me. "You must be freezing! The draft alone is enough to keep Santa's workshop covered in snow."

His arm encircles my waist and little goosebumps rush across my skin. Thank goodness the dress is long-sleeved.

"Grandma, grandma! Uncle Tom's angel is here!"

Tom leans over and whispers in my ear, "Out of the mouths of babes… speaking of babes…" He steps back, holding my hand up. "Wow. Just… wow."

I'm pretty sure I'm blushing. That or I've just stepped into a sauna. My whole body is warm all over despite the cool breeze from the open door.

"So this is the girl." An older woman steps into the hall-way. "That famous Cookie who wouldn't meet her signifi-cant other's parents. She finally decided to show up for Christmas."

Whoa. This just got serious.

"Cookie, meet my Mom, Lynn. Mom, this is Cookie, but I think it's best you call her Claire."

"And she can call me Mrs. Chamberlain."

Mrs. Chamberlain's eyes narrow as she looks me down and up. I get that warm feeling again, but this time it's not the nice version. After all Tom did for me last night, I've barely stepped through the door and I'm already blowing it.

Cookie is going to have to up her game.

"Pleasure to meet you, Mrs. Chamberlain."

"Hmmm. Likewise, I suppose."

She's not going to make this easy.

TOM

"So," I dare to ask the question, "what do you think of her?"

I want them to love her and I want them to hate her. If they hate her, then our fake breakup will go over a lot easier.

But after the dinner we've all just shared together, I want them to love her as much as I'm starting to love her.

Crap. These fake relationships need a warning sign. I tilt my head and catch sight of Claire playing with the kids. She's great with them. She's dressed like a bombshell but has no qualms about getting on the floor to play Go Fish.

That's my kind of girl.

"She passed every test," Mom says, taking another piece of pineapple. "I made every effort to be rude, condescending, and standoffish. She didn't waver from the picture of politeness and she's downright friendly. She just might make the grade."

Coming from Mom, that's huge.

"I don't know…" Leave it to my sister, Jen, to throw a wet blanket on holiday splendor. "She's awfully skinny."

I smack her on the arm.

"What? She is."

"Hi." Claire appears at the door to the kitchen with a shy smile on her face. Nothing about her was shy last night at her big event. I love seeing this other side of her. "I was hoping I could help with the dishes."

"No need," Mom goes scowly again, "you are a guest here. Guests shouldn't be doing dishes. It's an affront."

She's going rather far now. "Mom…"

"What kind of name is 'Cookie' anyway?" Mom crosses her arms. I know she's playing around, but when is she going to end the charade?

Oh yeah, in two years, if the last - real - girlfriend is any evidence. It's part of the *charm* of my family.

But how can I take this away from her? Mom loves this stuff. She lives for being the protector of her little son, her last born. And considering how she came back from the brink of death, who am I to stop her from having a little fun?

I did warn Cookie - Claire! It's all getting muddled in my head now.

She knew what was coming. Still, Mom is in her element.

"What kind of self-respecting girl allows herself to be called 'Cookie'? When Tom described you as independent, intelligent, and stunningly beautiful, I had a hard time marrying that up with 'Cookie'. How could you let him treat you that way?"

"Uh…" Claire looks to me for guidance, but I genuinely have no idea how to help her.

Maybe this is why I haven't brought any of those short-term girlfriends home. It takes commitment to endure this.

Her eyes light up. "It seemed like a cute nickname. Given all the names that Tom deals with on a daily basis - Fluffy, Missy, Cornelius - I figured that Cookie was just part of his lexicon." She flashes me a winning smile. I know she means it to show that she's holding up her side of the bargain.

But I am melting inside.

I made Cookie up. So I thought. When Mom and Jen pushed me to share more about my pretend girlfriend, I described the girl of my dreams.

And now she's standing in my sister's kitchen.

Mom looks at me. "I can buy her explanation. You're the odd one with the penchant for wacky nicknaming. Remember how you called your father Papalops?

I roll my eyes. "Yes, Mom. I remember. No need to share all the family secrets now."

Claire laughs and something inside me flip flops at the sound of it.

"Cookie, Cookie!" My niece comes running in. "Come play Go Fish, just one more time!"

Claire rests her hand on my niece's head. "Only if you promise to tidy your room like your Mom asked you."

"Okay, I'll do it."

Claire winks at Jen and then runs to join the giggling children in the living room.

"Yep." Mom nods. "She's a keeper. Even your father is a fan."

I peek around to see Dad with a demure smile on his face as he watches Claire with the kids. Normally Dad would be fast asleep in the Lazy Boy by now, that's his M.O., but he starts up another conversation with Claire instead.

All of a sudden, I get this giant block of concrete feeling in my stomach.

I wanted them to like her… but not *that* much. If they get too attached, they'll be devastated when we have to break up. And that was never part of the plan. I wanted to reassure them that I was doing okay, and most of all not reveal the great lie of the past two years.

But if they like her even just one hundredth of how much I like her, then this break up is going to be bad, bad, bad.

Mom and Jen are in deep conversation now about how kind Claire is, how sweet, how considerate…

"Hold onto this one," Mom says. "Not many like her."

I can't let this continue. I can't break my mother's heart, not after all she's been through already.

Claire made it clear, this is a temporary relationship with a purpose. She's got to be all set for that promotion, and I've not disappointed my family.

As for my feelings for Claire?

They are irrelevant. I can't let that get in the way, not now. So what if I have a little crush? So what if I've never felt so happy to not be reading veterinary journals every evening in slippers like an old man?

That was just a dream. A woman like Claire needs a man who is on the move.

I am not that guy.

I'm just a man who loves his family and is content to stare down the ears of canines and felines and rabbits alike.

I see the hope in Mom's eyes. It's best I put an end to this *now*.

"You know…" I saunter over to Mom. "She does clean up nice, I'll give you that. But I'm not sure it's going to work out."

I hear gasps from both Mom and Jen.

"What?"

"Are you crazy?"

I frown. "I guess the two of you like her even more than you let on."

"She's amazing!" Jen declares. "She got Cassie to agree to clean her room. She's practically a saint!"

I swallow hard. Claire has made a heck of an impression during the last few hours. "She has some real drawbacks."

"Like what?" Jen gives me that look, the one where she's the older sister and I'm an idiot.

"She's..." That's it. I just have to lie. There's no other way around this. "Everything is about her own progress at work. She never considers how it affects me. Her ambition is driving us apart. She works many late nights with rich guys and at big parties. How can I trust her when she's always putting herself in situations like that?" Okay, I'm on a roll now. "This has gone on for long enough. It's Christmas, so I can't do anything about it now, but I just can't picture spending my life with someone as selfish and self-centered as her."

Mom and Jen are staring at me with their mouths wide open.

"What? Why are you looking at me like that? All I'm saying is that I can't stay in a relationship with someone as egotistical as Claire."

Jen clears her throat as I hear a voice behind me.

"Tom?"

I close my eyes. Tell me she's not standing there. Tell me she didn't hear everything I just said. Tell me she knows I made it all up...

I turn around and the downtrodden look on her face tells me everything.

What have I done?

"Mrs. Chamberlain," Claire blinks and I can tell she's fighting back tears, "thank you so much for your hospitality. I haven't eaten so well in a long time. Jen, you're a great host." She turns around and calls into the living room. "Mr. Chamberlain, kids, it was a delight to meet you."

Don't go, Claire. Please.

But I can't make the words come out of my mouth.

"Stay!" Cassie throws her arms around Claire's knees. "We were having so much fun."

Claire pries herself free, with great difficulty. "I'm afraid I have to go." She practically runs for the door, grabbing her coat on the way.

"Claire!" I call out. Thank Father Christmas, my voice is back. "Wait." I run to the door, but she's already on the driveway. "It's not what you think."

"Let's leave it at this, huh?" She tries to get her coat on but her arm is stuck and she can't get it through the other side. "I wouldn't want to burden you with any more of my selfishness, after all. My ambition can be a real buzzkill. I get it."

I can't bear to watch her struggling with her coat anymore. It's freezing and she's going to catch a cold. And I'm hoping she'll stay.

"Please," I whisper in her ear as I help her navigate the coat. "It's not what you think."

"Please," she repeats back at me. "I've been dealing with men who can't handle my ambition my whole life. I don't need another one." Her coat firmly in place, she bows her head slightly. "Thank you for your help yesterday. I believe we can now consider our arrangement finished. Feel free to tell your family that I'm the selfish jerk who dumped you just before Christmas. Clearly, that's what you think of me already."

She spins on her heels and marches to her car.

"Claire…" I manage to say, but it's too late. Her car door is closed and the engine is starting up. She's gone before I can think of anything else to say.

What have I done?

When I turn back to the house, Jen and Mom are standing in the doorway, expressions of worry drawn across their faces.

"It's all for the best," Mom says, opening her arms.

I don't remember the last time I needed comfort from my mother as badly as I do right now.

CLAIRE

"Don't look at me like that."

It's the morning of Christmas Eve and Cornelius is giving me the look. I know he's judging me with those adorable bulging brown eyes.

I stuff my face back into the pillow. "You don't understand, Corny. You weren't there! It was humiliating. He called me selfish and self-centered. I heard it all. And he had no reason not to say what he really thought to his family. We weren't scheduled to break up for another week."

The phone dings.

Amelia: *What the heck happened last night?????!!!!??????!!!!*

How does she know? Amelia is like a magnet, pulling information from my head.

Me: *We finished up our arrangement. Too complicated. I'll tell you later. How do you know anything about it?*

"Come on, Corny. Let's get you a treat."

That was the magic word. He flies down the little steps I put beside the bed and is in the kitchen in half a second flat.

I grab the bacon-flavored stick from the jar on the extra-high shelf. Given that Cornelius prevented any intruder by howling from the time I left until the time I returned, he deserves it. And I owe my neighbors a big box of Christmas cookies for putting up with it. He's not used to being on his own.

"It's just as well you weren't there, Corny-boy. It was not a pretty sight. I just might have set you on that mean vet-head to teach him a lesson. Though that would complicate your annual rabies shot."

Ugh. Tom is still Cornelius' vet. I might have to change that, but Amelia wouldn't like it.

My phone dings again.

Amelia: *Not buying it. At work for Christmas Eve shift and Tom is a mess. Caught him mumbling to himself about being an idiot.*

Well, he deserves to call himself an idiot. Serves him right.

But… an idiot about what? This was always a temporary deal. That's what he wanted, the confirmed bachelor, as Amelia called him.

Me: *I got too caught up in the story. Should have seen through him. You were right, I had to protect myself.*

Cornelius is jonesing for a walk, so I suit him up in his ugly Christmas sweater (because sausage dogs deserve ugly Christmas sweaters, too) and out we go.

The crisp winter air feels like starting a new life. One where Tom Chamberlain isn't consuming my every thought as he has done for nearly the past week.

Except that he is.

I can't help imagining him with me now, strolling down the street as Christmas is finally upon us. There's a light dusting over everything, like a blanket of magic has covered the city. The Christmas fair is bustling with activity, which sets Cornelius into protector mode. The life-size elf cut-outs are as bad as the mall elves.

"Quiet, Corny! They aren't real."

"Isn't he just an adorable little boy!" Mrs. Claus says. Because Mrs. Claus is real and she's standing right in front of me, Christmas cap and red coat, right out of the movie.

"He's cute, but clearly has been traumatized by elves in a past life."

She looks me knowingly in the eye. "Don't we all over-react sometimes?"

Wait, is this woman the *real* Mrs. Claus?

Because she's looking at me like she knows what happened last night. And as for overreacting...

No, he called me selfish. He called me ambitious. He said I was egotistical. All this, and we were going to break up in a week anyway! Why'd he have to bad mouth me to his family just before we were fake breaking up from this fake rela-tionship?

"Mrs. Claus, I don't think you understand. If someone comes out of nowhere and insults you, how can you possibly consider staying friends with that person, never mind some-thing more?"

"It came out of nowhere, you say?"

"Out of nowhere!"

"And he would have no reason to say such things, perhaps even to lie to cover up his true feelings?"

"It wasn't even a real relationship anyway!"

Why on earth am I telling Mrs. Claus all of this?

...Oh wait.

Another reason why Tom would say such things, a reason that had nothing to do with me...

I look up at Mrs. Claus.

"Think about it..." Mrs. Claus says as she strolls back to Santa's workshop and hands out hot cocoa.

The pieces start to fall into place.

He needed this fake relationship so that his family

wouldn't think badly of him, because his mother had been sick and he couldn't bear to break her heart.

I had won her over by the end of the night. I saw through her meager attempts to be cantankerous and biting. It was all a show. She liked me.

And Tom was going to have to tell her we were breaking up. That would have been so hard for her after finally being happy her son had found someone he cared about.

I get it.

He and I were about to end this fake relationship. He *had* to badmouth me, make it seem like this relationship wasn't so great, prepare her for the breakup that was inevitably coming.

Because it was all fake.

The relationship wasn't real.

But my feelings are.

TOM

Christmas Eve and I'd rather climb into a hole and not come out until at least spring. Those groundhogs know where it's at.

Instead, I'm at my sister's place, watching Christmas cartoons where one of Santa's reindeer falls in love with a horse. We're at the part where the horse runs away because he can't believe that someone as special as Santa's reindeer could love him.

But lo and behold, Dancer is devastated that the love of her life has called her "too fancy, too plancy, too dancy" to love him.

Heaven knows what "plancy" means, but I'm feeling a whole lot of empathy for this sad horse.

I pushed Claire away.

I saw that look in her eyes, the joy at being with my family, the laughter that sparkled in them over coffee. The look of possibility, of all that could be between us.

I felt her lips on mine at the Huxton Christmas.

And then I let her leave.

She left, and I let her believe that I thought she was all

those awful things I said last night. Who's the plancy one now?

"Tom?" Jen puts her hand on my shoulder. "Your eyes are shining in light from the fire."

Because I ruined the best thing I've had in years before it even started.

She sits on the armrest. "Thinking about Claire?"

"Thinking about how I'd give anything to see her walk through that door right now." I stare at the fire. "I got it wrong. I got so much wrong. So much I didn't say, and I should have."

"It's never too late…" she turns her head away from me, toward the big bay window where the Christmas tree is twinkling.

"It is. I can't call her now. I've hurt her too badly. She couldn't possibly bear to see me on this of all days."

"Tom…"

"Best just to let it go. Live and learn. Enjoy Christmas with all of you."

The doorbell rings. Jen leans over and whispers in my ear.

"You get the door."

"Me?"

Cassie and Jim are up from the floor, running to the door, shouting on their way, "It's Cookie! It's Cookie!"

It can't be.

"Kids!" Jen screeches. "Get back in here! Uncle Tom needs Cookie time alone!"

I'm living in a dream. A Christmas dream.

I open the door to find Claire, her hair a giant mass on the top of her head, her cheeks rosy in the cold, and her eyes shining.

"Claire."

"Tom."

"I'm so-"

"Don't say it," she stops me. "I understand now. I understand everything. But here's the problem."

Problem. I should have known.

She looks at me with those deep brown eyes and I don't know if my knees are going to keep holding me upright.

She bites her lip. "We broke up, the fake relationship is over."

"That's right," I manage to whisper.

"But I like you *for real*."

I might faint. "I like you, too. For real."

"Can we try this, for real?"

"That's all I've thought about since this fake relationship began."

And then she smiles, everything in her radiating joy and by golly, this is the best Christmas I've ever had.

I take her cold cheek in my hand, and I kiss her.

For *real*.

The fog of our breath mingles in the cold air. She shivers.

"Let's get you inside." I put my arm around her and it feels like mistletoe and eggnog and fruitcake all at once. Just before we cross the threshold, I stop, savoring this moment that almost didn't happen. "Claire. My *real* girlfriend, Claire."

"Please…"

She has that gleam in her eye that makes me melt despite the cold Christmas Eve air.

"Call me Cookie."

THE END

EPILOGUE - CLAIRE

"Hang on, Cornelius!"

Tom's second honk is gentle but noisy.

"Coming!" I run to the window of my second-floor apartment and playfully shout my threat. "It's bad enough that Cornelius is yapping away at me, if you keep this up, you just might not get your midnight kiss!"

"Time's a-ticking!" Tom gives me that million-dollar smile that makes my heart beat louder. "Is Cinderella going to make it in time for the sparkly ball to drop?"

A quick glance up and my argument is solid. "It's barely gone six. I'll be out in a sec!"

Another voice calls out a window. "Don't go! This is highly entertaining, even better than those Christmas movies on the women's channel."

My neighbor, Trinity, has a bad habit of listening in on the many conversations Tom and I have had through the window in the past week.

But I can't blame her, we *are* shouting where everyone can hear. If I lean out far enough, I can see Trinity peeking out the window below me.

"Happy New Year, Trin."

"And you, fair neighbor. Catch you on January first!"

A dab of lipstick and I'm at last ready to make my appearance. Cornelius looks at me like I'm crazy for having let Tom wait so long. I might be projecting this onto him, given that he is a dog and not necessarily aware of the dating norms of us human types… but this is Corny, and judging humans is his favorite pastime after tearing apart plushy toys.

I slip-slide my way to Tom's all-wheel drive with Cornelius in my arms. He's being extra picky today about snow touching his belly. It doesn't matter that they cleared it this morning.

"Hi!" I say as a gust of wind sends my hair in all directions. It looked so cute a moment ago and now it's turning into a tornado of copper-colored flames. It's not a good look. I try to tame it and realize that Tom hasn't said a thing. I look up, and his mouth is open, his eyes fixed on me. "What is it?"

"You're…" He swallows. "You're beautiful."

His tone is sincere and sweet, and I almost can't handle it. No one has ever given me these feelings before, not like this. "Thanks. Ignore the hair. Nothing a ponytail can't fix—"

"Leave it. It's gorgeous. Wild and natural."

"Wild and natural. That's not a side of me I like to show much."

"I know." His eyes crinkle and he cups my cheek in his hand. "I want to know every side of you." He leans over and kisses me. Warm lips that gently brush mine, tentative and tender. He sits back into his seat but I feel like all time stopped.

It's like that every time.

I almost don't believe this is happening. When did my life take a detour into a dream world?

As we pull up to Tom's sister's house, Cornelius jumps against the window with his tail wagging.

"Did that Irish Setter catch your eye, buddy?"

Tom leans over and tries to look through the bit of window that Cornelius isn't covering. "Ah, that's Maggie. Cornelius has good taste. She's as sweet as Irish Setters get, and has the pedigree to boot."

I look at him with sly eyes. "Do you know all the girl dogs this side of the Rockies?"

He shrugs. "Girl dogs, boy dogs, puppies and elders, all through Hampton Falls. I know them, they know me. I might even be a household name. But enough of that, dinner and a couple of rug rats are waiting for us."

Tom's niece and nephew scream as they fly out the front door.

"Cookie!"

"And she brought a doggy!"

Within half a second, 'Cookie' is no longer the focus of attention, it's all about Cornelius. And he loves that. I put him on the ground and he leads the kids back inside like the pied piper.

The warmth inside is like slipping into the middle of an apple pie. Tom's dad takes my coat.

"Thank you, Mr. Chamberlain."

"So lovely to see you again, Claire."

It's a relief to hear my real name. This 'Cookie' alter ego is just fine for now, but I'm looking forward to transitioning back into Claire.

Mr. Chamberlain turns and calls in a voice deep enough to make the foundation rumble.

"Jennifer, Lynn, Doug! Cookie is here!"

Okay, so my real name hasn't fully caught on yet.

"It's so nice to see you again, Cookie dear." Mrs. Chamberlain pulls me into a stronger hug than I expect. In fact, she's crushing me. How does one get out of this gracefully? "I can't tell you how much we have been looking forward to seeing you again. Getting to know you better. Hearing more about how you and Tommy have spent these last two years." She finally releases me. "Our Tommy is a secretive one, but we're just so thrilled to have finally met you and we want to hear *everything*."

Uh oh.

How will that story go?

Oh yes, it all began when our mutual friend introduced us so that we could lie to my colleagues and his family, mostly with the intention of not hurting their feelings after years of lies, but also so that I could advance my career with some handsome veterinarian arm candy...

I give Tom a look and see as much panic in his eyes as in mine, except that he has a smile plastered on his face.

Smile, Claire. Don't let them see you sweating under this velvet new year's dress. What was I thinking? Never mind *see* me sweating, soon they'll *smell* me coming.

Now say something normal. "Of course, Mrs. Chamberlain."

"Call me, Lynn."

"Lynn, of course, Lynn." Must lighten the tone. I laugh.

Well, that was a weird sound that just flew out of my lips.

In my head, it was a giggle to fix the mood—well, my mood. But instead, I sound like something between a donkey and a hyena.

"Are you all right?" Tom comes to my side.

"I think I swallowed the wrong way." Sheepish smile. Hand on hip. Brush hair behind shoulder.

Why does everything feel so awkward! Is it just me?

Jen and her husband, Rex, guide us to the table, which has been laid out to the nines. Gold candles are the only light, and even the kids are on their best behavior as though the magic of one year turning into the next has instilled a volume switch in them. They're still tugging at each other's clothes, but they're doing it quietly.

"You look white," Tom says behind a napkin.

"I don't think the napkin comes with soundproofing."

His nephew shouts, "You're not *kissing* behind there, are you?"

Tom drops the napkin. "And what if we were?" He turns to me and makes a silly puckered up face as though he's going to land one on my cheek.

"Ew!"

Tom stops. "Naw, I'll save it for midnight." He squeezes my knee under the table.

I'm starting to feel a little better.

Ham, seasoned rice, sauteed vegetables, and these amazingly delicious chestnuts later, we're ready for that home-made chocolate cake awaiting us on the window sill.

"Let's clear up and I'll make some tea to have with dessert." Mrs. Chamberlain stands.

"Don't you worry, dear," Mr. Chamberlain sets a hand on her shoulder. "You ladies relax. Tom, Rex, and I will sort out the clearing. In fact, I've prepared a little something for you. If you all take seats in the living room, I'll bring it out."

I'm full enough to sleep until next year but the smells of chocolate cake and the crackling fireplace make me want to enjoy every single second.

"Come along," Mrs. Chamberlain puts her arm through mine. "Now that the gents have the clearing under control, you can tell us the *real* story behind you and Tommy. Isn't that right, Jen?"

"I want all the details." Jen winks at me.

There's no sign of maliciousness in it, but I feel the blood draining from my head. I glance at Tom just in time to see he's again no better than me. But I'm whisked away like a princess from outer space who is forced to colonize earth but runs into humans who demand to know her origins on pain of death…

I might be getting a little too dramatic.

We settle in, Jen and I on the cushy sofa and Mrs. Chamberlain in the arm chair like the queen of the house.

Do I lie? Do I keep up the story? I don't know what other options I have. If it were *my* family… well, for starters, I wouldn't have lied to them. At least, I have no reason to.

But then again, I have secrets of my own that I haven't revealed.

I can't blame him for having done everything to keep the peace in his family, especially when his mom was sick. After all she's come through, how could I possibly break her heart now?

"Here you go, ladies."

Mr. Chamberlain passes a tray of three glasses filled with what can only be cream liqueur. A little sniff and there's no doubt. I bet it's truth serum.

Tom steps into the room, his discomfort is written across his face. "Anything else I can get you?"

"No, Tommy dear," his mother waves her hand. "You get back in the kitchen so that the ladies can chat."

He blinks, staring at me wistfully before biting his lip and leaving the room. I can see the child in him, the one who fears his big old lie is about to come crashing down on his head.

"So…" Jen takes a loud sip and I take a mouthful of the liquid divinity – gosh, this stuff is good, I better be careful! – and she turns to me. "Tell us everything."

I know my answer. This is *his* family. I have to try not to lie.

While not telling the truth either.

"You already know the whole story." I wave my hand like

it's all no big deal and take another too-big-a-mouthful of the liqueur.

"That's not true at all!" Mrs. Chamberlain cries. "He tells us nothing. And yet *two years* you've been together. Have I got that right?"

First chance I've got – don't lie and don't tell the truth.

"Really, he's told you *nothing*? That's shocking!" I giggle, fortunately more humanlike than the last time. "That's my Tom, keeping things hush-hush."

I look from mother to daughter and I can tell.

They aren't buying it.

His mother wrings her hands. "I imagine you know there were times I have not been well these last couple of years."

"Yes, Tom told me." And that's the truth.

She nods. "My son. He'll go to great lengths to protect me. He has this foolish idea that he owes me –"

"Not just you," Jen adds. "He feels that way about all of us. All because he needed us when he was little. He hasn't seemed to grasp the idea that we all did what we wanted to. We *wanted* to be there for him. There was never any question, and there was never any indebtedness about it."

I put my hand on Jen's arm. "You all mean so much to him. The world. He'd do anything if he felt it would make you happy."

Mrs. Chamberlain sits back in her chair, a look across her face that I can't quite define…

"He'd even invent a pretend girlfriend for two years, wouldn't he?"

Uh oh.

My heart has just stopped. The sweat is starting again. My eyes are glazing over and I'm worried I might faint. What does the look on her face mean?

"It's okay," Jen puts her hand on my arm now. "We've always known."

"You did?" I take a gulp of the liqueur.

"Please!" Mrs. Chamberlain laughs. "From the start I had my doubts, and then, just as we were feeding the kids these giant chocolate chip cookies and I ask the name of this famous girlfriend, he looks at the kids' hands and shouts 'Cookie!' Ha! That boy. He always was a terrible liar."

"That's a big part of his charm." Jen winks.

"But... but..." I'm trying to get my head around this as the sounds of dishing clinking in the kitchen tell me the men are still hard at it.

"I'll be honest," his mom shakes her head, "I had no idea who was going to turn up at Christmas. I thought he might find some paid girl online –"

"Mom!" Jen shrieks.

"Not like that! Like on one of those social websites or something."

I try to mask my shock. "Paid girl? I hope you didn't think I was a 'paid girl...'"

Please say no. Please say no.

Mrs. Chamberlain smiles. "No. But I could also tell there hadn't been two years behind the two of you either. The way you looked at each other, the way you blushed and the way he tripped over his words when you were around, it was like..."

"Puppy love," Jen adds with a knowing smile.

They knew. They knew all along. I can't tell what this feeling is now, somewhere between relief and horror that we put on such an act when they saw through it.

Wait.

Puppy love?

"Cake!" Tom enters with the cake cut in neat little slices. "The first slice goes to my lovely Claire."

His mom leans forward. "Don't you mean 'Cookie'?"

"I just... I don't call her that *all* the time... it's just a cute name, you know? Maybe now we can call her Claire is all I mean."

He really is a terrible liar. And it's terribly cute.

"They know," I whisper to him, hoping he gets my meaning.

"They know what?"

I look at Jen and Mrs. Chamberlain, who are soaking in this moment like cats who caught the canary. Yikes, I need a better analogy than that.

"They know. About *us*."

"Of course, that's why you're here."

"Tom." I stand up and put my hand on his chest. His heart is beating like mad. "They knew all along."

"About…" He can't get the words out.

"Your fake girlfriend?" Jen pipes up. "Yeah, we did."

He drops the cake.

"Somebody grab Cornelius!" I shout out. "Chocolate is deadly for dogs!"

"Got 'im," Rex calls from the kitchen.

"But… but…" Tom looks between us all as his father rushes out to clean up the cake.

"Come on," his mother laughs. "*COOKIE?* And that hair-brained story about meeting her on a dock where her heel caught? We saw that movie *together*, you crazy snowflake!"

"But… but…"

"It's okay," I whisper in his ear. "It's going to take time to get used to it, but we can finally let Cookie go. I'll just be Claire from now on."

"And thank goodness," his mother adds, sipping on her liqueur like a queen in her armchair in front of the fire. "I far prefer Claire over Cookie."

"I, for one," Jen lifts her finger, "am a big Claire fan. Forget Cookie!"

"I don't understand what's just happened," Tom looks like

me like a little boy, but the panic has been replaced by a joyful glint, "but I'm pretty sure it's good."

"Very good," I tell him, snuggling into his chest.

"Quick, quick!" Rex comes running into the living room with the kids who were clearly asleep moments ago. He turns on the TV and the shining ball is making its way down. Everyone huddles into the middle of the room

"Ten, nine, eight..." we're calling out in unison, arms around each other.

"Seven, six, five..."

I look up at Tom beside me and catch sight of a tear as it rolls down his face.

A tear of joy.

"Four!"

He looks at me.

"Three!"

I smile, and I mean it.

"Two!"

He rests his cheek against mine.

"One! Happy New Year!"

His lips kiss mine, a kiss that can only be called the most honest kiss we've ever had. Cornelius weaves between our feet, his little tail whipping against our ankles.

Tom picks him up and snuggles us both in close to him.

"Happy New Year, Tom."

"Happy New Year, Claire."

THE END

Would you kindly consider leaving a review for Faking Christmas Love at the Doggy Spa? It makes me so happy to see all those shining stars - and more importantly, it helps other readers to know you enjoyed the book.

And the stories have only just begun!

Remember Amelia, who is determined to focus on her entry to vet school? Never mind love, and certainly not with the man she loves to hate…

Pick up "Hate to Love the Inspector" on Amazon for Amelia and Rob's story!

BIG HELLO FROM ELSIE

Hi! I cannot tell you how excited I am to share the world of the Dog's Paw Dog Spa with you. As the proud owner (and humble servant) of a happy Golden Retriever named Missy, I have fallen in love with the antics of various breeds and personalities.

But more than that, I am in love with love.

I've written lots of different types of stories, but after months and months in a hard lockdown (I live in France) I had to escape into my imagination, to a place where there's a happily ever after with a furball at their side.

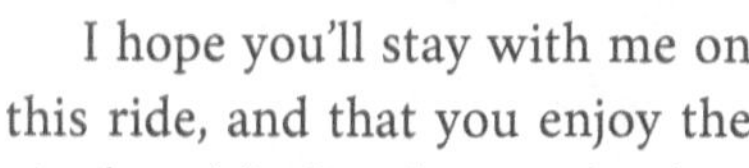

I hope you'll stay with me on this ride, and that you enjoy the giggles of finding love at the doggy day spa!

~Elsie

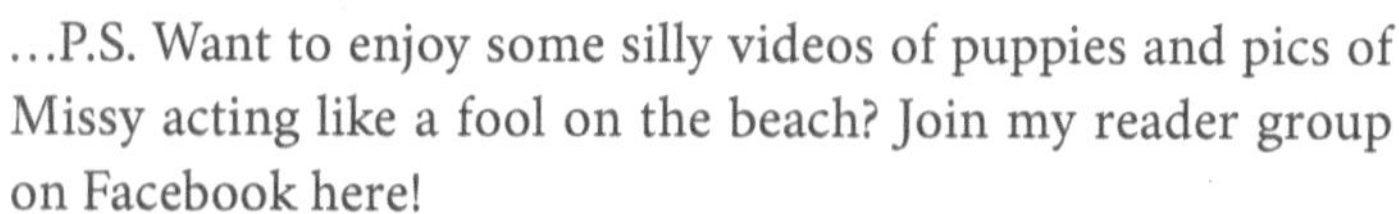

…P.S. Want to enjoy some silly videos of puppies and pics of Missy acting like a fool on the beach? Join my reader group on Facebook here!

https://www.facebook.com/groups/elsiescorner/